D0936692

Advanced Praise for *Dark Black*

"Reading *Dark Black* is like watching a night snowfall gather over a small-town streetlamp: it's gentle, gorgeous, haunting, and often eerie. But there are things hiding in the dark too—and Weller knows just when to unleash them."

—DANIEL KRAUS, co-author of *The Shape of Water*

"Haunted and haunting, these are stories of a past long gone and yet still with us. Stories of windswept plains towns, of a lost country, full of nostalgia and dread, romance and horror. At times, Weller plays with form (the experimental essay, the rock-band profile) to tell classic tales in new ways—while in other pieces he gives us the goods straight-up. And he has a knack for the mysterious and lyrical ending, coming sooner than you expected, catching you off-guard and wanting more."

—CHARLES YU, author of *How to Live Safely in a Science Fictional Universe*

"In the tradition of Ray Bradbury's classic collection, *The October Country*, Sam Weller's *Dark Black* took me on a gripping, gothic journey that I didn't want to end, even as I feared what awaited me beyond the next curve. Weller, a two-time Stoker Award recipient and Bradbury scholar, knows the genre and explores it masterfully as well as chillingly. With stunning illustrations by Dan Grzeca, this book is a keeper."

—DAVID MORRELL, author of *Creepers*

"As an English kid of the 70s I would collect and devour those little Pan books of horror, cheap paperbacks crammed with various short stories complete with tacky horror covers. I adored them. I didn't even realize how much I missed them until I started reading Sam Weller's mini-yarns, willfully losing myself in their minutiae and building unease with all the submission of an anxious little kid. Sam Weller is a one-man compendium, effort-lessly spewing out bite-sized tales of dread and singlehandedly dragging those tales of my childhood snarling into the present day. Horror short stories are where magic lies, tight enough to compel, brief enough to tear through should one fail to grab you. And I hope to see Sam Weller become the new face of the succinct horror fable."

—GINGER WILDHEART, front man of The Wildhearts, author of *Songs & Words*

"It's no surprise that Sam Weller, a renowned scholar of Ray Bradbury, would be such a beautiful storytell-er in his own right. What IS a thrill is the depth and breadth of *Dark Black*'s tales—some of which deserve to be read aloud, crackling-campfire style; others meant to be savored slowly and quite gloriously alone. By turns haunting, mysterious, wickedly funny and deeply insightful, *Dark Black* is a truly mood-flipping, mind-tripping collection."

— GILLIAN FLYNN, author of *Gone Girl*

Published in the United States by Hat & Beard Press, Los Angeles, California
FIRST EDITION

ISBN: 978-1-7327345-4-8

Art Direction by JC Gabel
Cover and Book Illustrations by Dan Grzeca
Book Design by Sabrina Che

These stories first appeared in the following publications: "Conjuring Danny Squires," *Chicago Reader* Fiction Issue (2013); "All the Summer Before Us," *Newcity* (2015); "The Girl in the Funeral Parlor" *Shadow Show: All New Stories in Celebration of Ray Bradbury* ed. Sam Weller and Mort Castle (2012); "Song of the Cicada" as "A Song for my Father" in *Chicago Tribune Printer's Row Journal* (2014); "Böse" *StokerCon Anthology*, ed. Michael Bailey (2018); "Night Summons," *Rosebud* (2012); "Roadside Cross," *Amazon Storyfront* (2013); "The Peephole," *Criminal Class Review* (2013); "The House They Used to Live In," *Arcturus* (2016); "The Shadows Behind the Trees," *Byliner.com* (2012); "Weird" *Chicago Tribune Printer's Row Journal* (2014); "Live Forever!," *All-American Horror of the 21st Century: The First Decade*, ed. Mort Castle, (2016). All other stories are original to this publication.

www.hatandbeard.com

19 20 21 22 23 LSC 10 9 8 7 6 5 4 3 2 1

DARK BLACK

STORIES

SAM WELLER

Illustrated by
Dan Grzeca

HAT & BEARD EDITIONS │ LOS ANGELES

For Jan—
My light and my love

"Death is the central factor in life."
— *Truman Capote*

TABLE OF CONTENTS

Little Spells

THE INFAMOUS CLUTTER HOME FROM TRUMAN CAPOTE'S CRIME CLASSIC *IN COLD BLOOD*

Literary tourists have an unprecedented opportunity to vacation in one of the most infamous locations in book publishing history! Now available to rent for the very first time—River Valley Farm—once owned by the Herbert Clutter family, prominently featured in the 1966 literary true crime classic, *In Cold Blood*, written by renowned author Truman Capote. Stay in this beautifully maintained 5-bedroom, 3-bath, 3600-square-foot classic mid-century farm home in charming Holcomb, Kansas. Marvel at the perfectly maintained kitchen originally designed by Mr. Clutter, gather at the fireplace where the family celebrated Christmas and many family milestones! The 1967 film, *In Cold Blood*, starring Robert Blake and Scott Wilson, was filmed on this very location as well. Celebrate American literary and cinematic history with a week-long stay (shorter stays not allowed) in this impeccably maintained late '40s ranch-style home. No pets, please.

The description of the house on VacationHomes.com grabbed my attention. It was literary serendipity. I had been laboriously scrolling through thumbnail pictures of crappy rental properties across the country for forty-five wasted minutes. All I wanted was a remote little house to finish the book I had been working on for far too many years. I am a full professor in the MFA program at the University of Central Indiana. Four times, my essays have been runner-up selections in the esteemed *Best American Essays of the Year* anthology. Immodestly, I am a bit of a star in academic circles and in the world of the experimental essay. I have written three books and edited four anthologies.[1] In 2010, my paper, *Hybritic Self-Reflection: Retaining Empathy in the Age of the Selfie,* created a mega-stir at the annual Associated Writers Conference in Austin, Texas. That same year, I read a portion of my book-in-progress at the Breadloaf Writers' Conference[2]. Jhumpa Lahiri[3] approached me afterwards and told me she thought it was "dazzling."

Still, my unfinished book was causing me considerable consternation. For starters, my course load had increased to a ridiculous 2/2. What were the administrators thinking? Do they know who I am?

I was under contract with Dartmouth University Press and the deadline loomed like a Category 5 hurricane spiraling offshore. I was working with legendary editor Gardner Fischbach[4] and there was no room for an extension. If I didn't turn my collection of connected essays in on time, I would be in breach of contract. The stress was daunting. Things got so bad, my GP acquiesced and generously dispensed a Costco-sized prescription for Clonazepam. Coupled with a single-glass of top-shelf gin every day at 5 pm, and I genuinely felt more relaxed. And this newfound composure afforded me a confidence that, in re-

---

1   *I, Brooklyn* (Harcourt Brace, 2002), *Pastiche* (University of Iowa Press, 2004), *Flowers of Ponderance,* (University of Texas Press, 2011); Anthologies: *The Last American Essay,* co-edited with Carefree Pimpleton (University of Iowa, 2006), *The God Colloquy,* co-edited with Philip Lopate (University of Iowa, 2010), *New Algorhythms* (Wake Forest University, 2015), *The Secret Goldfish* (New York University Press, 2017)

2   Breadloaf is the mother of all writers' conferences. Held each summer since 1926 outside Middlebury, Vermont. *The New Yorker* deemed it "the oldest and most prestigious writers' conference in the country." Everyone from Toni Morrison to Robert Frost have taught workshops or read their work there. I was quite honored to participate.

3   It pains me that I even have to footnote this, for fuck's sake, but for those who do not know, Jhumpa Lahiri is the Pulitzer Prize-winning author of *Interpreter of Maladies,* among many others. She also won the National Humanities Award in 2014. It saddens me how ill-read so many Americans are. They can list the entire filmographies of no-talent actors, yet have no clue when it comes to writers or books.

4   There is no need to explain this man's credentials. LEGEND.

turn, gave me the idea to find a worthy writer's retreat. So, I went to VH.com and started scrolling through rental properties, hoping one might be conducive to brilliance.

This is when I found the Clutter family farm.

In Cold Blood[5] is an undeniable tour de force of reportage, new journalism, and narrative nonfiction. Granted, it doesn't do what my peers[6] and I pull off in experimental memoir and the experimental essay but, still, it's a remarkable book for what it is. And Capote was often in the Clutter house when he worked on the book (and later to visit the film set). I figured, if I needed a place for a week or two, at a goddamned steal no less, I would have a sort of brush with the atoms of literary greatness. It was Truman Capote, for Chrissakes. Besides, I was on sabbatical and on book deadline. So, I clicked "Book It!" and the house was mine for a two-week run. I must say, I was more than a bit elated.

After that, I began researching the house and was intrigued to discover that it was reportedly haunted by the ghost of Nancy Clutter, the sixteen year-old daughter bound and shot point blank in her upstairs bedroom. Mr. and Mrs. Clutter, along with Nancy and their son Kenyon, were murdered in the house late in the night on November 15, 1959, but, as the paranormal urban legend goes, it was Nancy's ghost that still wandered the house, restless, agitated, seeking answers to her tragic demise.

~~~

---

5   *In Cold Blood* was published in 1966 and was instantly hailed a masterpiece by many a critic. It was also immediately controversial. Capote claimed to invent a new form—the "nonfiction novel," setting out to tell a meticulously reported story utilizing the tools of the fiction writer, i.e.: scene, character, dialogue, point-of-view, etc. He also utilized a simultaneous triple narrative structure. If Capote "invented" anything, he certainly birthed the true crime genre. And this is by no means a slight to the quality of the prose. *In Cold Blood* is elegant and elegiac, beautifully articulated, while utterly painful in its American Gothic grotesqueness.

6   When I say "peers," there really is only a dozen (at best) absolutely exceptional writers of experimental creative nonfiction currently at work in the field today. Most contemporary nonfiction essayists are overly concerned with narrative at the expense of structure and forms such as the lyric, braided, acrostic, or other hybrid essays.

A few weeks later, I was driving up the long, muddy lane to River Valley Farm in my Hyundai Kona. It was late in the day and growing dark, the evening light like an analog film negative. Heavy rains had slowed my drive. The rain had abated, but fog now billowed across the narrow dirt road. Only a few of the Chinese elms lining the straight dirt drive, planted by Herbert Clutter, still survived. Nearly all were dead or dying. The few remaining trees were now gnarled, arthritic, almost prehistoric.

Then I saw it to my right, through the opera house curtains of mist and darkness—River Valley Farm. The infamous Clutter family home.

The house, a 1948 two-story frame and brick affair, reposed on a large expanse of Bermuda grass. There were two adjacent corrugated steel barn-like buildings (as well as a number of old farm vehicles and dilapidated automobiles[7]), but the house was what really took my attention. It looked nearly identical to the old photos I had seen; exactly the way it looked in the 1967 film. Capote had been here, as had actor Robert Blake, who played Perry Smith, one of the two murderers. As I drove up, it was not lost on me that Blake himself was tried and acquitted of the 2005 murder of his wife. I thought about Philip Seymour Hoffman, who played Capote in the 2005 film, *Capote*. Hoffman won an Oscar for it, but then died of a drug overdose less than ten years later. As I parked my car I also knew, through my fastidious research, that the Clutter home only had three owners since the murders and one of them had committed suicide—albeit not in the house, thank God.

Adding to this mounting morass, Capote long maintained that writing his book led to his complete unraveling, to his downward spiral into alcoholism and drug use. While *In Cold Blood* made him one of the most famous authors in America, and rich, he never finished another book.[8]

---

7   All the cars and farm vehicles out by the two large steel storage structures gave the property a slight *Deliverance* vibe. It was creepy. I wondered if the house was better maintained, after all, I was paying for it.

8   I was facing my own brick wall with my current book under contract, well understanding Capote's crippled creative process. In my life, I have been crippled by my own dark past and it does come in to play into one's ability to produce art on demand.

I turned the engine off, doused the headlights, and pondered if the Clutter house was, perhaps, cursed.

The rental agency left the front door light on for me. They had informed me by email that the house key was under the black rubber door mat, kindly labeled "Welcome!" As I fumbled with the key, I heard the distant wail of a train and wondered if it was "The Chief," "The Super Chief," or "The El Capitan," as Capote had described the passenger locomotive wraiths roaring by in the rural night.

I unlocked the front door and stepped inside through a small vestibule and into the living room. Immediately, I thought of a famous photo of Truman Capote standing in this very space, the very space I was now in. In the photograph, he is near the painted white fireplace mantle, contemplative, wearing an olive trench coat, hands deep in its pockets. I must admit, it was overwhelming. I was in a mythic setting, little changed in over half-a-century.

I unloaded my car: my luggage, a box of books[9], my laptop, and groceries. I had also stocked up on several bottles of Tanqueray Ten gin. It was now completely dark, an early autumn night fallen upon far western Kansas. Once everything was inside, I closed the door and felt unusually alone, in this house with its horrors; this house more than a mile outside the outskirts of tiny Holcomb; on a large parcel of shadowy farmland; at the far end of nowhere. It felt like I was at the end of the earth, at the end of the spiral arm of the galaxy.

Then, a noise. It came from the basement. A sharp clicking and a small expulsion of air. I hoped it was just the water heater igniting, but I was on edge. The basement was where Herbert Clutter and his son Kenyon were tied up and killed.

I foraged through my Dopp kit for my anti-anxiety meds. In the kitchen I poured a glass of booze and popped a pill. The kitchen was like traveling in

---

9   I brought a mix of reference books (I still prefer old-fashioned dictionaries over the internet), along with a range of canonical and contemporary works for inspiration. Here is the God's truth: If you are a writer and you don't read, you should quit. Now.

the Wayback Machine. The white cabinets and blue and white tile counter tops were all original, designed by Herbert Clutter.[10] I filled a highball glass with ice and a generous portion of gin. I knew that in ten or so minutes, the edge would be gone.

A loud noise upstairs. Something had fallen. I'll admit, at this point, I was shaking. But I breathed. What did I expect? I came to this house, knowing its violent past, even hoping against my own common sense and total disbelief for some sort of paranormal encounter.

I started a self-guided tour of the house.

The master bedroom was on the first floor, along with the dining room and the office.[11] I decided I wasn't going to go down to the basement. There's just something about being all alone in a house (especially *this* house) and going to the basement at night. No, that could wait until sun up.

I went upstairs, acutely aware that Smith and Hickock had ascended these very glossy oak steps to murder Mrs. Clutter and young Nancy, the darling of Holcomb. I discovered what had caused the noise—an upstairs window was left open a few inches, the cream lace curtains shifting in the night breeze, ghostlike. The wind apparently knocked a small vase of dried flowers off a display table and it crashed to the floor.

No ghosts, I thought. Just the wind.

---

10   Herbert Clutter designed the house in 1948 and built it for $40,000. The home, by farmhouse standards, with two wood-burning fireplaces and 3600-square-feet on two floors (1700 additional square footage in the basement) was roomy and quite modern. Clutter was a fairly prosperous farmer. He was founder of the Kansas Wheat Growers Association, and was appointed by President Eisenhower to the Federal Farm Credit Board in 1953. By all accounts, Herbert Clutter was an outstanding family man and member of the Holcomb community. He was also instrumental in helping to build the Methodist Church in Garden City where the family would later have their funeral service.

11   SPOILER ALERT: If you have not read *In Cold Blood* and are unaware of the seemingly motiveless murder of the Clutter family, read no further. The first-floor office belonged to Herb Clutter and was the reason Smith and Hickock came to the house in the first place. Hickock, a convicted felon, had been told by a former cellmate, and former employee on the Clutter farm, that Herb Clutter kept a safe in his office with $10,000 cash inside. This is what brought Smith and Hickock up the long drive to the Clutter home that night. There was no safe, no cash, Smith and Hickock only left with $50, a pair of binoculars, and a transistor radio after having murdered the four members of the Clutter family. But the deaths of this family, because of Capote's book, continue to captivate people. Two older Clutter daughters, no longer living at home at the time, survive to this day but do not grant interviews.

Breathe.

I inspected the upstairs. Three more bedrooms, the murder rooms of Mrs. Clutter and Nancy. The four-post beds were both made up, with handmade quilts and frilly pillows. The bedside tables had doilies on them. The décor was precious and elderly, but warm and inviting despite the cloud of tragedy. I thought about where I would sleep in this house. I was unsure.

One thing that was updated—the living room had a large, high-definition flat screen television with a satellite hook-up. I sat down on the floral print sofa, glass of Tanqueray Ten in hand, and turned it on.

The TV came to life.

Channel 2: The first image was of a man, eyes wide open, lying on a sofa, a bullet hole in his forehead. It was one of those *48 Hours* unsolved crime programs.

I sipped my gin and pressed the arrow up button on the remote control.

Channel 3: An image of dozens of Syrian rebels, lying in heaps on top of one another, faces contorted because of a nerve gas attack.

I flipped the channel again.

Channel 4: Michael Myers crashed through the louvered closet door, kitchen knife in hand as Jamie Lee Curtis cowered in the corner.

Channel 5: Close-up of a screaming baboon, screeching, baring its teeth.

I turned the television off and finished my drink. I poured another.

There was one more oddity of modern convenience in this time-capsule domicile—internet service and two surprisingly thunderous wi-fi speakers. The owners had taken care to add a few amenities for renters. So nice. I pulled out my laptop and streamed the Rolling Stones. The anxiety meds had kicked in, and emboldened by the gin, I was feeling better. More relaxed. Fuck the ghosts and the noises and the past. I was here to write, dammit. I was going to finish what I already knew would be my magnum opus.

I cranked the music up. I blasted the Stones for a long time and continued to drink. What the hell? It was my first night there. It was getting late and the writing could wait until morning. Mick Jagger called into the night:

Kids are different today
I hear ev'ry mother say
Mother needs something today to calm her down
And though she's not really ill
There's a little yellow pill ...

As I stood in the living room looking out the picture window, drinking, reveling in this moment of total freedom, out in the inky darkness, headlights approached up the long drive.

What the hell? It was eleven at night.[12]

The lights bucketed up and down as the car dipped and lurched up the bumpy dirt road. My first thought was of Smith and Hickock coming up the driveway in their black Chevrolet in 1959. Who the hell was this? I am vehemently against guns, but at that moment, I wished I had one. Oak Lane runs parallel to the front of the house, then begins to snake towards it. As the car wheeled around, headlights played through the windows of the Clutter home, blinding me briefly, casting distended shadows across the living room.

Then the headlights went dark.

I heard a car door slam shut, soon followed by footsteps up the walkway and the two concrete stairs to the front door.

A knock. I was fucking mortified.

The music roared. Mick was now proclaiming:

---

12   Reading up on the house before my arrival, I learned that gawkers, gapers, and voyeurs frequently drove up Oak Lane, the long dirt lane towards the Clutter farm, for a glimpse of the infamous home. People had flown drones over and filmed it. There seemed to be no end to the curiosity surrounding the Clutter family murder, and this is one of the reasons the current owners decided to rent the house out on VacationHomes.com. I hoped that my own visitor was just another of the curious throng of inquisitors.

Pleased to meet you

Hope you guess my name

I turned the music down.

"Who is it?"

"Holcomb police," a raspy voice responded beyond the front door.

How could I be sure it was really the police? Here's the most absurd thing: I'm in a house where four people had been murdered and there wasn't a fucking peephole in the front door? Had no one thought to install this simple mechanism of modernity?

"Is there a problem?" I responded. I was feeling loopy on the booze and meds, my cranium now a carnival tilt-a-whirl.

"Is everything okay in there?"

"Yes. Why?"

"Do you mind opening up the door?"

What the fuck? Really?

"Sir, excuse me, you understand it seems reckless to just open the door to a stranger. I'm renting this home."

"I'm Officer Dunphy, Holcomb, Kansas P.D. This house was vacant for two months. I noticed the lights were all on and wanted to make sure everything was in order."

Oh, what the hell? I reached to unlock the door. Copycat murders happen, but I was done with this little game. If it was a cop, I'd done nothing wrong. If it was some killer emulating Hickock and Smith, well, fuck it. He would have to face me, at this point an angry and utterly inebriated Fulbright scholar.

I opened the door.

Officer Dunphy was young, with a military air. He was over six feet tall, muscular as a monster truck, topped with a crew cut. He wore a dark blue uniform, a silver badge, and a chest radio.

"Evening," he said.

"May I help you?"

"Sir, do you have proof you're a guest here? Holcomb is a small town and we had no notice the home was available to rent."

"I have an email confirmation," I said. "If you look at VH.com you'll see the house is available for rental."

"VH.com?"

"Vacation Homes dot com."

He looked over my shoulder.

"Mind if I step in, sir?"

I stepped aside and he entered and glanced around. The Stones still played, albeit at a much lower volume.

"I have the owner's phone number, if you'd like to call her," I offered. "She can confirm everything."

"How long are you staying here?"

"Two weeks."

"Why would you rent this house? Don't you know about it? Or does that sort of thing interest you?"

"I'm a writer, officer. This house has a tragic past, but it's a literary one." I realized I was slurring my words. I usually didn't drink more than one glass of gin with the anxiety meds but I had violated my own rule and was feeling the effects.

Officer Dunphy walked in to the living room, looking around curiously.

"You write books?"

"Yes."

"Do people still read those?"[13] he asked, moving into the dining room. "I've never actually been inside this place. This is where it all happened."

I nodded. "That's why I decided to rent it."

---

13   This is what is wrong with America.

I opened the rental contract up on my laptop and tried to show him.

"Here's my agreement," I said, balancing the computer in my hand. He didn't even look at the screen.

"The owners of this place are really private," he said, as he walked into the kitchen, looking at every detail. "Gawkers come here to take pictures. The owners put up no trespassing signs, they would even fire guns into the sky when cars drove up, if you can believe that, to scare off strangers."

He ran his hand along the countertop.

"Mind if I have a peek in the basement?" he said, finally looking at me. "I'd love to see it."

"Sure."

He opened a door, flicked a light switch on, and descended the staircase. I wasn't going to investigate it earlier, but now accompanied by Officer Dunphy, I was no longer as intimidated.

We reached the bottom of the steps. The walls were cinderblock, there was a forced air furnace, a water heater, and in the corner, a few cardboard boxes marked "X-Mas Ornaments," possessions of the current landlords. Next to these was a large plastic Santa Claus lawn figure, the kind that lights up. It was standing against the wall, looking right at me, right through me.

Officer Dunphy walked around the basement with purpose. He inspected one of the walls.

"Huh," he said.

"What?"

"I read on the internet there was a blood stain down here. It happened when Perry Smith stabbed and then shot Mr. Clutter.[14] The stain is near where his body was found. And here it is. I thought it was some urban legend."

I walked over and looked at the reddish-brown stain on the wall. I suddenly felt sick to my stomach, not so much by the apparent blood, but the mix of

---

14   The murder scene for the 1967 movie was also filmed in the basement.

alcohol and drugs in my system, and a sense, for the first time, of how violated the Clutter family was. It was horrendous and I was contributing to it.

I vomited. It splattered over the concrete floor.

Officer Dunphy stepped away from me. "What the fuck? Are you okay?"

I wiped my mouth with my shirt sleeve. "Yes. Just feeling a little overwhelmed."

"Looks like you've been drinking, too. I'll let you clean your mess up there," he said, pointing to my puke. "Then you should go to sleep."

"I guess so."

"First," he said, pulling out his cell phone. "Would you mind if I take a few pictures down here? It's pretty incredible."

"Whatever you want. I'm going back upstairs."

I returned to the living room and sat down on the sofa. Officer Dunphy paraded around the house with his cell phone, taking photos of each room like an eager tourist in Hollywood with a map to the homes of the stars. I was feeling sick again and lay down.

"Hey, thanks for letting me see the house," he said, finally emerging in the living room.

My face was pushed against the cushion of the couch. I couldn't even get up.

"You don't want to see my rental agreement? I thought that's why you came out."

"No, I believe you. What I can't believe is that I just toured the Clutter house. It's incredible. Absolutely incredible!"

He walked to the front door to leave. He turned to face me. "Hope you feel better. You should really lay off the sauce."

He closed the door behind him and I fell asleep.

I woke the next morning in the same position. I had completely passed out. The skies outside had cleared, and sunlight fell all across River Valley Farm. The land was awesomely flat and went on forever.

~~~

My first night had been a fucking abomination. Today would be better. I made coffee, then went to the basement to clean my mess from the night before. I showered, dressed, and dedicated the rest of the morning to writing.

I didn't write a word. Well, I wrote several paragraphs, but deleted them. They were all shit. I sat there for the entire morning crafting nothing. I made breakfast. Went for a walk across the farm, and tried to write after lunch. More garbage, far beneath my standard.

I drove into town. There was not much to see. Lots of industrial buildings, a concrete plant, tall grain silos, and countless steel storage facilities. A new elementary school. A convenience store. A bank. The police station. A Mexican restaurant. There was no town center, just train tracks cutting the town in half. I saw very few people. It felt soulless. A ghost town.

I drove back towards Red Valley Farm, up the gravel drive with the dead trees. I returned to the house with the intent of writing again. This time, what the hell, I poured a drink, despite the previous night.

I sat down in the dining room and worked on an essay that had been vexing me for some time, a prose poem about my chiropractor. For a few hours, I drank and wrote. I was stringing words together that felt good and right. But when you write and you are in the moment, in that groove of mystic meditation, it is virtually impossible to see the proverbial forest through the trees. You can't be sure if what you are creating is, in fact, any good, and you can only rely on what you are feeling. And I was feeling it, dammit. By the end of the day and a fifth of Tanqueray Ten, I had a complete draft, and I was buzzed and more fearless. I hoped that this night, when the rural land once again surrendered to shadowy underworld, I might encounter the spirit of Nancy Clutter, wandering the house.

I dimmed the lights, listened to the Doors, "The End," and sat on the sofa, and I drank. My writing was done for the day.

By 9:30, I passed out on the couch, out for the rest of the night.

~~~

Next day. Up at dawn. Brewed coffee and reread the 1,500 words I had crafted the previous day.

It was all complete shit.[15]

What was wrong with me? Why the anxiety? What the hell was going on?

I worked all morning, holding off on the booze. I am, if anything, disciplined at my craft. Phillip Lopate once told me that I was "as prolific as a Norway lemming."

The Clutter house was quiet, remote and lonely. It was the perfect setting to complete my book, yet I was in mental disarray. I was crafting drivel faster than a B-rate Hollywood film studio. What the actual fuck?

So, I opened the gin. I sat down on the sofa and opened the copy of *In Cold Blood* I had brought along. By page eleven, as I sat there reading and sipping my gin, I was reminded that Herb Clutter, by all accounts a good and generous man to all, including his farmhands, as Capote described him, only had one attribute in others that truly bothered him, a strong disdain for alcohol:

'Are you a drinking man?' was the first question he asked a job applicant and even though the fellow gave a negative answer, he still must sign a work contract containing a clause that declared the agreement instantly void if the employee should be discovered "harboring alcohol."

---

15 How does a writer know when his work is sub-standard? Can this level of immediate objectivity be taught? Reading is really the key, distilling the words of so many before us, subconsciously learning from the masters until their brilliance becomes ours. I plan on penning a book in the near future on the writing process.

~~~

Days moved by like the swipe of a finger on a smart phone calendar app. I was lost and producing a veritable cesspool of absolute waste. I don't believe in writer's block, but I was crippled. My creativity was akin to one of the last few remaining Chinese Oaks that Herb Clutter planted when he had life and time and the world before him.

And then, for him, it vanished by knife and muzzle flash.

Six days of super-glue stagnation and I needed a change. I was also out of booze.

I drove to Holcomb to replenish my gin supply. When Capote came to Kansas to write his book, Finney County was dry. Thank God that had changed.

I stepped into the convenience store, a birdcage bell above the door jingled to mark my entrance. A young woman behind the counter greeted me with an enthusiastic "Hi!"

She wore an acid-washed jean jacket with tassels, nodding her bob of chestnut hair. I had to look at her twice. She had a milk complexion and if Nancy had lived, she would look like this young woman. Almost exactly.

I moved down an aisle towards the booze. Most of the canned goods on the shelves were covered in a fine layer of dust.

I was dismayed to discover the store didn't carry top shelf gin, only bottom-shelf Carnaby's London Dry in a plastic bottle. But I grabbed it anyway.

"Is that it?" the young woman asked when I approached the counter.

"Yes, thanks."

The register pinged as she rang up my gin.

"I haven't seen you around here before."

"Just visiting," I said.

She looked at me. "Where you staying?"

I smiled. "At the old Clutter Farm. It was available to rent."

She cocked her head to the side.

"Oh, I see," she said at last.

"See?"

"You're one of them."

"Who? What do you mean?"

"The people who think the murders are cool. My grandpa and grandma knew the Clutter family. They were friends."

"I don't think that. Not at all."

"Well, it's sad."

I pulled out of the parking lot and realized the house was just not doing it for me. Holcomb, in fact, held little allure other than the history of Capote walking its streets in 1959, taking notes and a few photographs. Most of the locations he noted in his book were now long gone. But he had stayed in nearby Garden City, the town where the Clutters were laid to rest.

The sky was shifting into autumnal variations of flannel greys. I headed to Valley View Cemetery.

I found the graveyard in Garden City, a little over ten minutes from Holcomb. It was larger than Holcomb and a proper city.[16] Thanks to Google maps and findagrave.com, I easily located the family. The internet is a strange amalgam of remarkable convenience and keyhole voyeurism I often have trouble reconciling.

I parked my car.

The sky had darkened as I walked out among the headstones and plastic flower bouquets toward the Clutter family plot. I approached the rose-colored granite. A light rain began to fall, more of a mist than anything.

Herbert Clutter, 1911-1959, next to his beloved wife, Bonnie Mae Clutter, 1914-1959. To the left, Kenyon, 1944-1959, and to the right, Nancy, 1943-1959.

I stood before the headstones. I was now residing in these people's home,

---

16 Holcomb has a modest population of just around 2,000.

the place Herb Clutter had designed and built with a future in mind. And, now, here I was, yet another stranger in their midst.

"I don't mean to trespass," I said, under my breath.

~~~

I couldn't fucking write in that house. I kept drinking and listening to music, my standard jumpstarts, but nary an original word emerged. This book was fucked. The deadline would be blown. Into my second week, I was destitute. I kept hoping in a sick way to encounter the spirit of a murdered teen girl and, instead, the only haunted spirit was my own.

I drank more. And took more pills. Because, why the hell not? It extinguished the flames of failure, at least in the moment. And I produced nothing, I wrote nothing. In my second week of residency at River Valley Farm, I drank and swallowed anti-anxiety medicine and listened to Johnny Cash sing about not taking your guns to town.

And late one night, a waxing crescent moon bathing the shorn rows of farmland beyond the house, I blasted Black Sabbath and decided to just get completely shit-faced. I was not writing. Clutter Farm residency almost over. Manuscript incomplete.

I went to the basement stairwell, flicked the lights on, and descended the stairs. They had filmed the murder scene for the '67 film here. The real murders had occurred here. I walked over and looked at the splatter on the wall. I ran my fingers over the cinderblock wall, across the stain.

We do things sometimes without thought, pure animal instinct, no intellect. I ripped my button-down Oxford shirt, blowing the row of buttons. I took my jeans off and my underwear.

I ran upstairs and poured a tall gin and gulped it.

Ozzy wailed: *"Oh no no please god no."*

And I opened the front door, stark naked, drunk, head spinning, and I ran. I ran across the dry Bermuda grass. I ran beyond the steel hut farm buildings and the old equipment and the dilapidated cars. I ran, naked, across the clods of earth and the rows of wheat stubble. I ran out into the night, under the sliver of moon, and kept on running.

I don't know how far I went. I could have run forever.

Finally, I collapsed, in the void of mud and rows of plowed field. I fell to the ground, in that area Kansans called "out there." I was naked. Filthy. Arms and legs splayed. Staring at the night sky. I clawed dirt in my hands and cried. I thought of the four shotgun blasts on that November night. I thought of Kenyon and Nancy, Herb and Bonnie.

Mrs. Bonnie Clutter. Capote described her as suffering from depression, from anxiety, from anguish. She had even sought treatment, he wrote. Mrs. Clutter's mental lapses into mania, Capote said, were her "little spells."

I saw so clearly now how the Clutter family had been victimized not just that night, but long after it. Capote was a goddam opportunist. He had turned their tragedy into his art. Robert Blake and Scott Wilson and Director Richard Brooks, they shot their film in the house, next to and even on the Clutter furniture. And then another film, *Capote*, awarding Philip Seymour Hoffman an Oscar.

And finally, the house went up for rent and a sad fucking writer side-saddled alongside the decades of opportunism and abject tragedy.

How many people had profited, marveled, been drawn in by the murder of this midwestern family? How many?

Laying there, out in a dry mud clod field I was having my own little spell.

I stared at the moon and I quivered up at a dark black sky.[17]

---

17   Editor's note: Near the end of his two-week residency in the Clutter family home, where this essay concludes, Alex Langman suffered an acute nervous breakdown. He was hospitalized at a Garden City psychiatric facility where he is still undergoing treatment. "Little Spells," the title essay in this collection, is his first piece of writing, penned while hospitalized, with permission from his doctors. We are hopeful Alex will make a complete recovery.

The Circumference of the Glare on the Patio

Monica has never actually heard real gunfire before. She certainly didn't grow up with guns in the house. None of her relatives hunted. No one in her family ever served in the military.

Sure, she's heard guns in the movies and on TV and even at her friend Jamal's house, in his messy basement, when friends gathered and vaped and many of the kids played shooting games, congregating around the PS4 like it was some mystical talisman.

But these shots, the ones she is hearing right now, right this very second, they are quite real.

Pop. Pop. Pop.

Three shots.

She is certain it is gunfire. How? It sounds like firecrackers. And, after all, every news report she has ever seen about school shootings, every single one of them, the survivors always said the gunshots sounded like "firecrackers."

She is sitting in her Applied Mathematics II course at Rock River Community College, alongside eighteen other drowsy students when it happens. It is hot in the room, the forced air heat cranked up way too high for a mild winter day. Outside, through the large windows, the sky is flannel grey and all the winter trees are bare and cold, the branches trembling in the wind.

Everyone hears the three pops, including Professor Adams who stops in the middle of scrawling a long quadratic equation on the dry erase board. Everyone is bored, but they all immediately sit up at the popping sound from somewhere off in the vast building. When Dr. Adams hears the noise, he turns from the board and looks at the students.

"What was that?" Eduardo Vasquez asks.

Everyone in the room is on edge. The energy in the class shifts in the instant, like someone has pulled a switch and charged the room with electricity.

"Sounds like fireworks to me," declares Dr. Adams, a concerned look upon his bearded face. He rolls the dry erase marker back and forth in his hand.

Monica stands up from her desk. Calm. She has rehearsed this moment many times in her mind. Doesn't everybody in her generation?

Get out.

She slings her book-laden backpack over her shoulder, grabs her winter jacket, and marches for the door.

"Ms. Jones?" Dr. Adams says.

"Y'all should leave, like, right now," she says as she moves between desks toward the door, the other students glancing up at her.

Wraithlike, Monica glides past the other students and straight out the door. She steps into the long and shiny hallway. At the forefront of her mind is exiting the building. Immediately. This was what she always planned to do if *it* happened.

Escape.

Why wait around? Why delay and then get stuck putting desks and filing cabinets in front of the classroom door? Why wait for the lockdown when you are, ostensibly, trapped in the building with an active shooter?

Nope. No way. Not going to happen.

The impossibly long hallway is empty. Quiet. Classes are in session. She steps out and looks all the way down, where the vanishing lines of the hall converge. This is when she sees him. A lone figure, dark, more shadow than man.

He is wearing all black. Bulky, something on his head, too. A helmet? Something over his face, maybe? It is hard to tell.

What is unmistakable is the gun. Long. It looks like it is baring its teeth. Menacing, even at this distance.

Get out. Get out.

Monica stands statue-like and watches as the man moves with purpose across the hall, opens a classroom door and enters. Then she hears an eruption of gunfire.

Pop. Pop. Pop. Pop. Pop. A mechanized monster. Syncopated. Frightening.

Monica turns and runs down the hallway in the opposite direction. She knows where the nearest exit is. She has rehearsed this all in her mind.

The lights in the hall go dark. Emergency flood lamps situated near the ceiling illuminate a halogen path down on the floor.

More gunshots. Pop. Pop. Then come screams in the distance. Back where the shots occurred. Pleading. Sobbing. It sounds like a chorus of anguish.

An automated voice booms over the college's public address system:

"There is an intruder in the building. Please take appropriate measures to seek safety. Repeat. There is an intruder in the building."

Get out. Get out. Get out.

She runs from the gunman, in the opposite direction. But the next sound is unmistakable. Doors up and down the long hallway automatically lock. All of them.

Including the exits.

Click.

Lockdown.

She knows now she is trapped inside. *Why do they do this? Trap people inside with a fire-breathing dragon?*

Pop. Pop. Pop. Pop. Pop. Pop. Pop. Pop. Pop.

She runs to an exit door and pushes hard on the horizontal silver bar. It doesn't budge, steel-clad immobility. The door has a vertical, slender rectangular window. Monica can see out to a large snow-covered area where, on warm days, students read, eat lunch, drink their Frappuccinos. On better days, days that now seem like some wonderful dream, she sat out there, too. It is brilliantly sunny outside with all the snow, the circumference of the glare on the patio, nearly blinding. How she wishes she could be out there now.

Pop. Pop. Pop. Pop. Pop. Pop. This time much closer. Locked in, she is now forced to hide, to seek refuge, to pray he doesn't come near her. She sprints down the hall to a staircase.

Pop. Pop.

A bullet strikes the wall close by, boring into the drywall. Has he seen her? Is he shooting at her? That was horribly close.

She takes the stairs up three at a time. She is young. She is strong. A swimmer. Yoga. At the top of the stairs on the second floor, she reaches the massive college library. An amalgam of new and old.

The new: Open. No doors. Tons of windows and natural light. Computers and technology and space for students to work and to commiserate. This is, in many ways, the college student center. Installations of student art are on display throughout. The library is spacious with many alcoves for students to work and hang out.

The old: Row after row of stacks. Shelves of good old-fashioned books towering to the ceiling. Like the athenaeums of yesteryear. A massive collection.

And a good place to hide.

She runs into the library. No one is at the front circulation desk. No student worker at the coffee cart. Everyone has hidden. Somewhere.

She runs deep, deep into the stacks.

Pop. Pop. Pop.

More distant gunfire. He is still down on the first floor.

Many rows in, she crouches down, surrounded by books. She grew up with books, *Harry Potter* and *The Hunger Games* and *Coraline*. Books make her feel safer, they bring her solace, despite this nightmare scenario. A fortress of books all around her. Knowledge and ideas and imagination. She stays still and she waits and she hopes that the authorities will arrive soon and the gunman is apprehended quickly or that he takes his own life as they so often do.

She thinks about the little children of Sandy Hook and how scared they must have been. Only in first grade. Why does this keep happening in our country? She thinks of the high school kids at Columbine. And the victims in Orlando, and Parkland and Pittsburgh and Littleton and ...

A metallic sound. In the library. There is no mistaking it. Shit. He is here. In the library. With her. He is changing the magazine on the monster. He clears his throat. Her heart is hurtling in her rib cage like it is falling through time and space down, down, down.

Breathe, Monica. Breathe.

She looks at the books in front of her. The books lined up on the lower shelves. She is in the 300s in Dewey Decimal parlance. The self-help section. The irony is not lost upon her. And then she begins to wonder if maybe she has a way around all of this. Maybe, perhaps, maybe she should try it. Utilizing her powers. Self-help and a little luck may be the only way out.

~~~

When Monica was still a baby, her parents suspected she had certain abilities. The first time they noticed things, she was barely old enough to lift her head. Monica was on her tummy in her crib. Mama had just fed her. She jangled the sterling silver rattle for her and the toothless little baby was transfixed by the sound, an angelic bell ringing inside the shiny object. When Mama had set the rattle down on a table next to the crib, Monica craned her lolling head up and looked at the silver toy beyond her reach. She stared at it and stared at it.

And then the rattle rolled off the small table and it dropped to the floor with a clang.

Mama turned and looked at her in the crib.

"Why, baby, if I didn't know any better, I'd think you just moved that rattle with brute mental force ..."

Several months later, when Monica was a year old, she was sitting in her high chair. Daddy was listening to Coltrane, as he so often did around supper time. Mama had served her carrots and peas that she grew without chemicals in her garden pots on the back porch. There was so much love in that little apartment it was palpable.

Then, as babies so often do, Monica flailed her little hands across the high-chair tray, sending tiny peas and baby carrots raining down to the floor.

"Now, baby, why'd you go and do that?" asked Daddy, laughing as he chased runaway peas to the corner, his heart in a constant state of love brimming over for his daughter.

Monica leaned over the side of her high chair and looked at the mélange of vegetables so far down on the scuffed oak floor. She stared at them. And kept staring. And then, as her Mama and Daddy looked on, the peas and carrots started to tremble. Moving ever so slightly at first, then, like a film in reverse, the peas and carrots flew back up from the floor and to the tray, landing where they had originated.

Monica laughed with glee.

Mama and Daddy turned to each other.

How did she do that?

They took her to see the pediatrician. Dr. Hansen was a no-nonsense doctor. She was at the end of her career, ready to retire, she had raised her own son as a single mom, she had seen just about everything and every ailment, disorder and anomaly a doctor can see over the course of a long and busy career.

"We suspect Monica can move things with her mind," Daddy explained.

Dr. Hansen took this the same why she would have taken a parent saying they suspect their child had an ear infection. She was expressionless. Cool.

She held a wooden tongue depressor in her thick hand and extended it to the child. When Monica reached for it, Dr. Hansen withdrew her hand, like a game of keep away. After a few seconds, she moved the tongue depressor closer.

"Do you want this, Monica?" she asked.

Monica swatted clumsily, trying to grab the object, but Dr. Hansen pulled it away from her again. The child looked perplexed.

Out of reach from Monica, Dr. Hansen unfurled her fingers, showing the little piece of wood, that old stalwart of physician's offices everywhere. Monica stared at the object intensely. And then it began to tremble in Dr. Hansen's hand and, like that, flew over to Monica, hit her little chest and quickly dropped to the floor.

Dr. Hansen said softly, "Lord, have mercy ..."

They took her to a series of specialists, Western, Eastern, Freudian, Jungian, and New Age. A diagnosis? They were all just guessing. Some dismissed her abilities altogether, calling it "trickery" and "hocus pocus." The consensus, however, despite the skepticism was that Monica possessed some sort of psychokinetic ability. "PK," they called it.

She could move small objects, lightweight objects, with her mind.

When she was twelve, Monica was at an arcade with a friend and found she could guide a wooden Skee-ball into the smallest rings at the top of the game, just by concentrating, earning one hundred points with each toss of the ball. The machine kicked out so many tickets for prizes that the manager finally came out and told her she had to stop. She was like a Vegas gambler on a winning streak who is asked to leave the table with their earnings. Monica was given a stash of candy and stuffed animals and stickers, one of everything in the arcade's glass case.

But then, like all pre-teens, puberty arrived and Monica's body changed and, much to her surprise, her telekinetic abilities started to weaken. And, then, they were gone. No matter how hard she focused on objects, she had lost her ability to move things with her mind.

And, so, here she is in the library at Rock River Community College in the middle of an active shooter situation. She is hidden many rows back in the stacks. There is a back exit out of the library, part of the reason she decided to go there in the first place. But this means she will have to leave her bibliophilic fortress, and move back many, many rows of stacks to reach the door.

As she sits there, crouching down, she hears a text message tone in the library. Not her cell phone. His cell? Someone is texting this shooter, this odious person, now, of all things? The sound was close. Two rows of shelves away? Three at most?

The text tone goes off on his phone again. He is closer. "Apex." She knows this tone. Standard and boring.

Monica peers through the open space above a row of books. She can see him. He is pacing like an agitated zoo animal down a row of books three stacks in front of her. He is holding the matte black monster. It is an AR-15. She has seen it enough times on the news. They all use it. He is dressed head to toe in black combat gear. Cargo pants with lots of pockets. He appears to have on a bulletproof vest. A helmet. Goggles. This guy came for war. He intends on lasting awhile and inflicting as much death as he can.

So why is he here in the library?

If he wants a high body count, would he really be hunting one lone student in the library? Or did he come here to reload?

Staying crouched low, Monica slowly, quietly spiders toward the end of the row of books, towards a break in the shelving, an aisle in the stacks. She peers out and can see the circulation desk. On top of it, a small box holds short pencils and another contains little scraps of paper. Students, even in this digital age, find these pencils and paper—throwbacks to another era—useful, and they appreciate the ease of scribbling a call number in their search for a book.

She stares at the circulation desk. At these little boxes. Totally focused. She wants to create a distraction. With all her might, all her concentration, blocking out everything, including her present pulsing fear, she looks at the little box of sharpened pencils on the circulation desk.

It moves.

It inches slowly to the edge of the desk. The paper box flips on its side and all the little pencil stubs begin tumbling out, like timber logs on a flat-bed after the chains have broken. One by one they roll out, clattering to the floor.

She peers between the books on the shelves. He turns. And he points the monster toward the circulation desk.

She makes a break for it, running down the aisle of books towards the back exit, her back hunched over and her legs pumping faster than she's ever pumped them. And as she is running, she thinks of the scrap paper on the circulation desk and, not even looking that way, but simply concentrating on the small squares of paper, she envisions them fluttering off the desk, pigeons in flight from their roost.

The papers respond. Like playing cards in a game of 52-card-pick-up, flying off the desk one after the other after the other.

The additional distraction gave Monica time to dash down the aisle. Eight rows of shelving to the exit.

Seven rows.

Six.

Five.

Four.

Three.

The gun breathes fire. Pop. Pop. Pop. Pop.

Bullets strike the metal stacks. He is shooting at her.

Two.

Pop. Pop.

One.

Pop.

She feels a bullet. It passes by her right ear. Barely an inch away. It strikes a book on a shelf, the binding absorbing the bullet as it shreds through the pages.

She hurtles down the back stairs, to a landing. She turns and hurries down another set of stairs. She reaches the first floor. It is empty.

Then she hears boots clacking behind her, striking the concrete floor in military precision. She turns and he is at the other end of the entryway, pointing the monster directly at her. She concentrates on its teeth. She thinks of the bullets slowing down as it sprays. She focuses all her being on this moment. Tries to slow the bullets, shift them away from her. She feels a graze on her arm. Another on her leg. She falls, and as she's falling, she thinks of Mama and Daddy and their love supreme.

Guided by Demons

There's good reason to believe that Guided by Demons, the pop-punk quartet out of East Los Angeles, is, perhaps, the most aptly named band in rock music history. That is, if the group's controversial and outspoken frontman Wanker (aka Paul Reeder) is to be believed.

One listen to the group's latest bouncy, fuzz-saturated, profane as a port-o-potty-sing-a-long single, "The Third Rail," (off their schizophrenic eponymous third album), and you might start thinking an exorcism is in order. Cling tight to your rosary beads and holy water, dear reader!

Songwriting credit on "The Third Rail," along with all eleven tracks on *Guided by Demons* (Warner Bros.) is given to Wanker and Tommy Neptune.

Yes, *that* Tommy Neptune. And before you go on saying that's impossible, I'm way ahead of you. So, I set out to get to the bottom of this story by sitting down with Wanker himself.

~~~

First, a bit of musical content: Tommy Neptune was the guitarist and founder of '70s punk progenitors, the Cry Babies. From 1976 to 1979, the Cry Babies released three massively influential records, prodding *Rolling Stone* to hail Neptune as "possibly the finest songwriter the punk genre ever produced."

Neptune took all the tropes of punk—the-rebellious snot-and-fist-cacophony, the ragged three-minute quasi-pop gem, along with the anti-establishment rage, and he damned near drove a bulldozer through the formulae. Ain't no verse-chorus-verse-chorus-bridge-chorus predictability to be found. Nope. Neptune's songs had few boundaries, yet they somehow worked, even finding their way to the U.S. Top 40 with 1978's "Rigor Tortoise."

"He was Dylan in a leather biker jacket," wrote legendary rock critic Lester Bangs, "with a rap sheet of drug busts and blown rehab visits to go with the Nobel Laureate gutter poetics."

Tragically, and yes, predictably, Tommy Neptune died in 2012 while touring with his solo band. Neptune was found unresponsive on his tour bus in a parking lot outside, of all stupid places, the Mall of America in suburban Minneapolis. It was a less than glamorous end—some proffered even pathetic—for punk rock royalty. A subsequent autopsy showed Neptune had a veritable and lethal Schlitterbahn of cocaine, ethanol, and methylenedioxyamphetamine coursing through his system. He was fifty-nine.

But now, according to Wanker, Tommy Neptune is back, apparently collaborating from the grave.

"These aren't some old, unreleased Cry Babies reject songs we finished and recorded," says Wanker. "People have done that shit with old Hank Williams compositions and crap. That's not what this was. Not at all. It's not like when Wilco and Billy Bragg took the journals of Woody Guthrie and put music to the found lyrics either. That's not how any of this worked," he says.

So how did it work?

"I wrote these songs with Tommy Neptune's ghost," says Wanker.

~~~

To fully understand this rock and roll tale of the dark fantastic, you must first understand (and an even bigger leap of faith—*believe*) Wanker, who is, frankly, an unreliable narrator at best. Still, it's damned hard to deceive the ears, and one spin of *Guided by Demons* and you are saddled with a holy-fuck realization: This is a brilliant extension of where punk music could and should go to keep the genre vibrant. The album elicits an auditory-induced trouser soiling—it's that good, that unexpected, even to this jaded veteran rock music critic. Wanker adds that his bandmates, Jon Jon Johnson (guitar), Mike Alvarez (bass), and Ballz Richthofen (drums) gave invaluable input on the compositions once the band was in the studio. But make no mistake, the new album is a Wanker and Neptune union, top to bottom.

"It's cool to collaborate with a legend," Wanker says. And he insists, there were no séances, candles, incense, Ouija boards, or other black magic paraphernalia employed during the making of *Guided by Demons*.

"Rock and roll is a powerful, mysterious force," he says, seated casually in the living room of his East Los Angeles home. The house is a modest single-story Spanish stucco affair, an oxymoronic setting of domesticity best summed up by the primary colored mélange of Fisher Price toy vehicles parked in the parched front yard, and the disquieting original John Wayne Gacy oil painting of a clown looking over the sofa where Wanker sits for this interview. Wanker is the father of a three-year-old son and an avid collector of artwork by serial killers. He claims to own an original "cypher" from the Zodiac Killer; he owns a charcoal illustration by *In Cold Blood* killer Perry Smith; and he has a framed, handwritten letter by H.H. Holmes.

Wanker has an extensive arrest record of his own—no homicides, mind you, but his past is littered with drug busts, domestic violence calls, and felony theft arrests related to a long-running cocaine addiction. In 2013, Wanker even got called out online by his own loyal fan base for borrowing money from them to support his drug habit.

"Look, man," he says, addressing this decidedly female journalist by the male descriptor, "you can choose to not believe me about collaborating with

Tommy Neptune," he says, gravel-voiced, taking an inhumanly long drag on an American Spirit cigarette and then slowly exhaling a cloud of nicotine that rises to the living room ceiling and just hangs there like a bank of noxious smog in the L.A. basin.

As this is a story about the deceased and, possibly, an otherworldly creative collaboration, it's worth noting that Wanker is cadaverous in his own right. He stands a striking six foot, two inches tall and weighs a mere 149 pounds. His skin is impossibly pale and slathered in tattoos. He dyes his spiky Sid Vicious coiffure matte raven black.

"I know I'm not the most credible of sources," he says, cigarette dangling from his lips. "But who fucking cares, man? Listen to the album! Just listen to it! Dude, I hope next time out I can write with Jimi Hendrix, Elvis, or fucking Tupac. Tommy fucking Neptune teamed up with me and the proof is right there on the record."

~~~

Tommy Neptune was born Thomas William Battersby, Jr. at precisely midnight, Easter morning, 1957, in Leeds, England. Son of an electrician and a pediatric hospital nurse, Battersby was an only child. His father, a champion alcoholic, a connoisseur of Irish whiskey, who was occasionally, by Neptune's later accounting, prone to brutal episodes of emotional and physical abuse.

"When I was eight," Neptune recalled in his memoir, *Guttersnipe* (Doubleday, 2009), "my old man was pissed at me for, like, not putting my toys away. Some stupid shit like that. He proceeded to hold my face over a pot of boiling water on the kitchen stove. The rising steam scalded me badly. I was terrified that he was going to submerge my face in that water. From that day forward, every fucking day, I fantasized about killing the old man. But I didn't have to.

Two years later, when I was ten, Jamesons took care of matters. He died in hospital of cirrhosis of the liver. Good riddance, you horrible, rotted, fuck maggot."

The little boy, the future punk progenitor and darling of the CBGB set, was raised by his widowed mother. An only child, he retreated to cartoons, comic books, the Beatles, the Stones and later, Ramones.

"Music brought me through everything," he said. "*Everything*. It was the only constant in my life."

By the age of eighteen, out of school, penniless, rudderless, working as an electrician's apprentice, Battersby met up with Leeds guitarist David Walls and it was, by all accounts, incendiary.

"David played like Chuck Berry with an M-80 in his arsehole. And he wrote songs that were just as explosive," recalled Neptune in his book.

Soon after, the duo was joined by Manchester drummer Mick "Gall Stone" McCormick and bassist Suzy Quaalude (aka Susan Berkowitz). The Cry Babies were hatched and, within a year, playing gigs in London clubs. Soon after, they signed to Looking Glass Records. In 1976, they released their first album, *X Marks the Spot.* Jaded and too-cool-for-school critics on both sides of the pond were all agog.

The band's run was short. Three records. Three years. A relentless touring schedule followed by the stereotypical pitfalls of rock and roll. But in their lightspeed run across the rock galaxy, the Cry Babies impacted punk music perhaps even more than the Clash or Ramones or any other band in the genre.

By late 1979 the band imploded amidst turmoil, infighting amongst the four members, near-fatal car accidents, arrests, addiction and all the tropes of clichéd rock excess. And they never reunited. Tommy Neptune went on to record six respectable, and at times brilliant, solo records, but he never achieved the same success he had had with the Cry Babies. Still, Neptune toured constantly. He played festivals, suburban clubs, punk rock nostalgia cruise ship extravaganzas—you name it. Purists lifted their noses, decrying Neptune as a sell-out.

"Go fuck yourselves, you miserable lot of weapon's grade Gobshite," he responded to his critics in a 2004 *NME* interview.

On January 12, 2015, his solo band overnighting in a Minneapolis Marriott hotel, Neptune chose to sleep in the rear bedroom of his tour bus.

"It was snowing in little icy diamonds that night," recalled Zack Jones, guitarist for Neptunes' solo band. "We had dinner with Tommy, a few cocktails, and before he went to the bus, I'll never forget, he looked at the snow and said it looked like cocaine falling from the sky. He had been trying to stay straight, but maybe the snow triggered him. We said goodnight, he climbed on the bus, did some blow, and that's the last time any of us saw him alive."

The Hennepin County Medical Examiner's Office issued a statement three weeks after Neptune's death concluding the punk legend died accidentally of mixed-drug toxicity—coke, ethanol, and methylenedioxyamphetamine along with a smorgasbord of other prescription meds in his system: Lunesta (sleep disorder), Clonazepam (anxiety), and Geodone (anti-psychotic).

Neptune's body was found in a fetal position, unresponsive, by tour manager Micky Simonson at 8:45 am on December 13. Simonson promptly called 911, and even as paramedics arrived on the scene, the tour manager took to Facebook and announced: "I have lost my best friend. RIP Tommy Neptune, 1956-2015."

His body was still on the tour bus, but thanks to social media—this generations' AP Wire—everyone knew Tommy Neptune was dead.

The music world responded instantaneously.

"If there is a fucking Mount Rushmore of punk," said Sex Pistols frontman John Lydon, "it surely has my ugly mug alongside Joey Ramone, Joe Strummer, and, of course, Tommy Neptune. This is just a stupid fucking loss and the universe can go and right fuck itself. Okay?"

"No one wrote songs like Tommy Neptune," said Blondie front woman Debbie Harry. "And no one ever will."

"Art alone endures and vinyl lasts forever," offered Green Day's Billie Joe Armstrong. "I refuse to accept this loss so I'm going to go listen to the Cry Babies and pretend like he is still with us because he always will be."

~~~

Tour bus rental companies often book a motor coach for months at a time. The bus can sleep up to twelve musicians and crew. Tommy Neptunes' bus had a master bedroom in the rear of the motorcoach, a queen bed, a wall-mounted TV and eight bunks in the middle of the vehicle (four on each side). The bus, a Prevost X3, had only 5,799 miles on it when it was booked for Neptune's seventeen-city 2012 tour. After Neptune's body was found on the motor coach, it was sent back to the rental company, Shining Star Coaches of Thousand Oaks, California. Like hotel rooms where famous stars die (you, too, can sleep in the room where Whitney Houston died!), the bus was cleaned and booked for a tour just two weeks later. And this is where Wanker and Guided by Demons meet at the proverbial crossroads.

"Bands don't get the massive advances to make records like they used to," says Wanker. "Guided by Demons hit the road to raise money to finance our self-titled album. Fuck A and R people and labels and all of that bullshit. We booked a tour with the goal to produce and release our own album without all the turgid corporate fucking puppet strings."

According to Wanker, this is when shit got real on the occult front.

"Our booking agents had a full-blown U.S. tour scheduled and secured a tour bus and driver."

What Wanker and the rest of the band members in Guided by Demons didn't know? The bus they were in was the very vehicle where Tommy Neptune had died just two weeks earlier.

~~~

Guided by Demons played a sold-out show at the historic Starline Ballroom in Carroll, Iowa. The band returned to their tour bus, post gig, for the requisite decompress.

"We were in Colorado two days earlier," said guitarist Jon Jon Johnson. "While we were there, weed being legal and all, we had purchased some edibles and stood out front of the bus, to hang with some fans before we pulled out to head towards our next gig in Chicago."

Wanker, focused and off drugs and booze, chose to forsake the parking lot soirée, opting to retreat to the bus. "He was feeling inspired and wanted to strum on an acoustic guitar and write some new material," said Johnson.

With the rest of the band standing outside in the Iowa cold getting baked, Wanker sat on one of the leather sofas on the tour bus and started to noodle and strum out chord progressions.

"I played a simple, repetitive riff, it just sort of emanated from me," he recalls. "Anyone who writes music or poetry or anything creative knows that feeling when you, the writer, is just the conduit for the art."

Seated on the sofa, guitar in hand, Wanker could still hear the muted voices of his bandmates laughing and talking outside.

"I kept playing the riff (the beginning of the anthemic first track on *Guided by Demons*, 'March of the Black Friday Zombies,') and I started to hum a little melody to go along with the guitar riff."

And that's when it happened.

"Someone started harmonizing with me—a man's voice, all nicotine, whiskey, and steaming asphalt, humming along to the tune I was playing."

Wanker stopped strumming his guitar. He looked over his right shoulder, then his left, startled.

"At first I figured it was one of the guys in the band, standing outside the bus singing along. But I realized it was too close, the voice was eerily right there next to me."

Wanker started playing the repetitive riff again, humming a melody line along to it.

"I heard that voice again, harmonizing with me."

He stopped strumming. He put the guitar down. Stood up. Peered out through the horizontal metal blinds. His bandmates were still outside, talking to a few fans.

"I thought someone was fucking with me, one of the guys in the band, or our tour manager," Wanker recalls. "But then I realized, whoever it was, they were singing an amazing harmony line to my melody. It was something I would have never written. I don't think the guys in the band would have come up with it either. It was unexpected, simple, yet original. I pulled my phone out of my pocket and opened up the voice memo app and started recording. I picked up the guitar and started playing the song again. This time I didn't sing, I just played the riff."

As Wanker recalls the scene, retelling it while seated on the sofa in his L.A. home, his three-year-old son ambles into the room. Cash Reeder, doughy with a mop of brown hair, walks side to side, sort of like the Stay Puft Marshmallow Man from *Ghostbusters*. He is shirtless and still wears a pull-up diaper. His cheeks are chubby and red and he smiles at his punk rock father as he walks across the room and into his waiting arms. It's a tender, unexpected scene. Wanker lifts the boy up, places him on his lap and kisses his cheek. Cash runs his tiny fingertips over a tattoo on his father's arm, a striking, photo-realistic image of the devil, replete with horns, a pitchfork, fire and brimstone all around him. For the past two months, Wanker has been flying solo, a temporary single-dad, his longtime-girlfriend Rachel Rose (Cash's mother) booked into an Arizona rehab center for a prescription pill addiction.

"She went all Rush Limbaugh on me with the opioids," he says. "I went into the wrong business," he laughs. "I should have opened an addiction and recovery center like that Passages fucking Malibu place. I'd be rich."

Wanker reads a Dr. Seuss book to his boy, and then continues to tell the story of co-writing an album with a ghost.

"After writing 'March of the Black Friday Zombies,' obviously, a lot was going through my mind. Was the voice I was hearing 'the muse' so many artists over the course of time have talked about? Was this the 'daemon,' as it was called by the ancient Greeks? I wasn't sure. But there was one thing I *was* sure about," Wanker emphasizes with complete sincerity. Whoever was singing melodies and lyrics to his chords and riffs, whoever was harmonizing with him, whoever was inspiring him, Wanker knew the voice.

"I knew right away, man. It was Tommy Neptune. I mean, I grew up listening to him, you know? No one would mistake Elvis or Michael Jackson if they heard them singing with them. If you heard Janis Joplin, like, suddenly singing in your kitchen, you'd know it. I knew Tommy Neptune was singing these songs I was playing. And he wasn't just singing, he was writing the songs through me. We were collaborating."

Wanker sat on the bus and wanted desperately to summon his bandmates in to experience this otherworldly visitation. But he was worried.

"I was afraid that if I stood up, went outside to get the boys in the band to hear what I was hearing, it might all go away. There was a certain Ju Ju goin' on and I didn't want to lose it."

So he kept recording on his cellphone and started playing a second tune, track two on *Demons*, "Suburban Subfugio."

"Again, I played the song all the way through without stopping," he says. "And Tommy kept right on singing."

When Wanker finished strumming the last, Gatling gun chords to the outro of the tune, he stopped, overwhelmed, overjoyed, incredulous.

"Is that you, Tommy?" he asked. "Is it really you?"

There was no response to the question, only silence, accompanied by the cackling THC-emboldened laughter of his Guided by Demons bandmates still gathered outside the bus.

"If it's you, Tommy," Wanker said, "help me write a hit single."

Wanker started playing the opening chords to "The Third Rail," simple, up-tempo, instantly memorable, a sunshiny pop opus.

"Tommy's voice came in and started singing the opening lines to the tune," recalls Wanker.

Blue snarl calling/acrid doped-up snarling/fingers around the jugular/leave me the fuck alone.

"I've never written a song that quickly," says Wanker. "It just poured out of me, like compositional diarrhea, except it was pretty, like a beautiful summer punk single with lyrics so deceptively dark it would have made Aleister Crowley put high-wattage light bulbs in his bedside lamps."

Quickly, Wanker had a trio of new songs recorded on his phone. The three members of Guided by Demons climbed onto the bus to find their frontman in a hopped-up state.

"He was definitely riding a gnarly wave of something," recalled Jon Jon Johnson. "Wanker has battled his coke addiction for so fucking long, I gotta be honest, we were all a bit concerned that maybe he had returned to his wicked ways. He's been sober for a few years now and none of us want to see him go back to drugs. Not with Cash. He has a son and good reason to stay clean."

Bassist Mike Alvarez and Wanker go back to their grade school days in East L.A. "I've known Wanker since he was learning his multiplication tables at Cesar Chavez Elementary and I'd certainly never seen the dude like that before," says Alvarez. "His pupils were totally fucking dilated, his voice seemed like the register had gone up a few notches. He was fully amped."

Wanker sat his band members down on the tour bus. "I told them in no uncertain terms that I'd just written the three best songs of my fucking life. I opened the app up on the phone and played the tunes."

Heads lowered, locked-in, the guys in Guided by Demons sat on the bus, focused like congregants at Catholic mass presided over by the Pontiff himself. When the first track concluded, Johnson was the first to look up as Wanker pressed pause on the recording app.

"Well?" Wanker asked, rhetorically. He already knew what he had—au courant punk-pop grandeur, gratis from a dead legend's collaborative generosity.

"That is a fucking amazing song," Johnson said. "It's avant garde, yet reels in at precise moments back to the core song structure. You nailed that. You really just wrote that while we were standing outside? Seriously, dude?"

"I did," said Wanker, proud, confident, feeling high on creativity and totally in tune to the flow of the energy in the universe at that very moment.

"I can't wait to hear the melody and lyrics you put to it," said drummer Ballz Richthofen. "That song fucking rocked."

And it was this comment that caused Wanker's ride atop the glorious crest of creativity to come crashing down.

"Whoa, whoa, whoa," I said to the guys. "Did they not hear the melodies and lyrics by Tommy Neptune? Could they not hear him? It was all right there on the damned recording!"

Guided by Demons sat on the tour bus and listened to the next two songs Wanker had composed and recorded. But the only one who could hear the contributions of the legendary, late, great Tommy Neptune was, indeed, Wanker himself.

~~~

The fifteen-city *Guided by Demons* tour rolled across the heartland of America and into the rust belt. Wanker was silently flummoxed that his bandmates couldn't hear his collaborator on his iPhone recordings, yet he was also buoyed. He had three new top shelf songs in the proverbial megabyte can for the band's forthcoming self-funded album.

As subsequent nights of the tour arrived like calendar pages flipping aside in an old movie, Wanker grew more agitated. Seated in his L.A. home, he describes his existential angst:

"Why would Tommy fucking Neptune's ghost write three songs with me and then fucking vanish like an apparition's flatulence in the wind?"

Every night, after every show, Wanker retreated to the tour bus, pulled out his guitar, hoping to reconnect with the spirit of Tommy Neptune.

Nothing happened. Cleveland. Philly. New York City.

"Nothing, man. No Tommy Neptune. I wondered if that was it. I had somehow channeled his spirit that one night and maybe it was over. I was desperate to connect again, to write more songs, to feel that incredible high one more time."

"We believed the entire Tommy Neptune story," says Alvarez. "We all believe in ghosts and shit. I mean, why not?"

The *Guided by Demons* tour ended in Lakeland, Florida, two weeks to the day after Wanker's supernatural encounter in Iowa. Wanker tried every night, after every gig, to resume contact with Neptune's spirit. This Sisyphean task, his desperation to have one more productive tête-à-tête with the punk legend drove him to actually start thinking about doing drugs again.

"The thought did cross my mind," he says. "Like Aldous fucking Huxley, I wondered if I needed something to open the doors of fucking perception. Something to reestablish contact with my deceased collaborator."

Yet every time Wanker thought about doing a line of coke, returning to his old ways, he pulled out a tiny picture of his son from his wallet. While we are seated on the sofa in his L.A. home for this interview, he withdraws his wallet and takes out the photo. It is weathered, creased in one corner, the color has faded a little, making it look almost like a Kodachrome throwback to a different, more innocent analog age. In the picture, Cash is seated atop an oversized fiberglass yellow cartoonish duck, one of those bouncy, spring-mounted contraptions in playgrounds for kids to climb on and sway back and forth. In the photo, the boy clutches handlebars, holding on. Cradling the photograph in the palm of his hand, Wanker looks down at his boy, smiling wide with pure delight, one of those simple, halcyon childhood moments.

"I can't go back to drugs, you see? When the urge strikes, and it really hasn't, up until getting stood up by Tommy Neptune's fucking ghost on further creative collaborations, I really had no desire. My son is my life."

After Guided by Demons had returned to Los Angeles post tour, Wanker decided to start writing more songs with similar aesthetics to the trio of tunes he had penned with Neptune. He would just have to go it alone. The three tracks he had composed with Neptune all had similar characteristics: time changes a-go-go; instantly memorable rhythm guitar hooks; meandering ribbons of melodic detours and resplendent tangents; unforgettably, anthemic choruses. This was toe-tapping punk rock—a Frankenstein's monster—part boot-stomping AC/DC riffage; rockabilly bombast; Motörhead relentlessness; skull and bones call and response choruses; Johnny Cash tales of failure, anger, redemption, and salvation.

With his son in a nearby daycare center, Wanker holed up in his house and endeavored to recreate the magic he had shared with the ghost of Tommy Neptune on that tour bus in the middle of somewhere Iowa.

"It was a miserable fucking failure," he says, with a heavy sigh. "You can't create that way. It just has to happen organically and I was trying too fucking hard, you know?"

Wanker spent two weeks trying to pen new tunes that sounded like the three he already had.

"Total fucking failure," he says.

~~~

Months went by. Guided by Demons had raised more than enough on their tour to self-fund the production of their next album. But Wanker was now afflicted with a paranormal-induced case of writer's block. And then one day at home, alone, sitting on his couch underneath the John Wayne Gacy clown original, he googled "death of Tommy Neptune."

The first link that came up was to TMZ, a prurient, celebrity trash gossip site. It shocked him. The article about Tommy Neptune's death in Minnesota showed a picture of the tour bus where the punk legend had died. Wanker stared at it. That bus, he knew that bus. He had just toured on it. He had written three songs with Tommy Neptune right where Tommy Neptune had gone off to that great, piss-stained, stickered up, smoke-laden punk rock club in the sky.

~~~

The Prevost X3 sped down Interstate 80. One driver and one occupant.

"I had nothing else to lose, man," he recalled. "Outside of going back to cocaine and using that to dislodge my creative block, I figured, what the hell?"

So Wanker booked the very tour bus he had travelled on earlier in the year. The bus where Neptune overdosed.

"It wasn't cheap, man," he says, ubiquitous cigarette hanging precariously from his lips. "A bus like that, with a driver, runs about two grand a day."

But Wanker looked at it as a worthwhile investment.

"Maybe, just maybe," he says, "I could reconnect one more time with Tommy Neptune by going to the very spot where he died."

With his longtime girlfriend, Rachel Rose, clean and home from rehab, Cash had a caregiver and Wanker loaded his guitar and headed towards Minneapolis, Minnesota.

~~~

The bus parked in the exact spot. On the parking lot fringe of the Mall of America. It was bone-chilling cold, even by Twin Cities standards. The wind chill was minus ten degrees. Wanker had sent his driver, a burly and balding employee of Shining Star Coaches off to a Cracker Barrel for dinner. He was alone on the bus on the very anniversary of the death of Tommy Neptune's passing.

"I dimmed lights, lit candles, did all that trite séancey shit," he said. "I was desperate, man."

He picked up his guitar and started strumming. What emanated forth was like nothing he had ever played before. "I played some weird chords, like augmented 7th shit, things I didn't even know."

He kept strumming, his phone recording every impossible note.

And then he heard it. The voice. All nicotine, whiskey, and steaming asphalt.

Wanker kept right on playing, recording eight tracks in a matter of just a few hours of spiritually guided prolificacy.

And when he was done recording the eighth tune, the epic closing track on *Guided by Demons*, "The Executioner's Bong," he knew that Tommy Neptune had left. For good. Forever.

"I could just feel it," says Wanker. "After I recorded that last song, he was gone. Totally."

Jacked up, exhilarated, triumphant, Wanker put his acoustic guitar down, put on his leather jacket and decided to step off the bus for a smoke and to breathe the cold Minnesota night air.

"It was a weird feeling, you know, man?" he says. "On one hand, I had just written an entire album with Tommy fucking Neptune. But then I had a scary realization ..."

Wanker was off the bus. He lit a match igniting the tip of his American Spirit cigarette. "I realized, man, that was it. I knew, somehow, that I would never write with Tommy Neptune again. Like, ever. I can't explain it. I just knew. And while it felt great that I had eleven songs, a new album's worth of incredible, transcendent, new tunes, I had a little bit of a freak out moment right there, in the parking lot outside of the Mall of fucking America."

Wanker dragged on his smoke. He stared off at the dark, looming consumerist mall in the distance, Mecca to Americans. His hands started to quiver.

"I had a fucking epiphany right there, man. It was scary. I would never write music like that ever again. Tommy Neptune was gone. I had just created my best work, thanks to him. That was it. I had peaked. The zenith of my career had just happened outside a disgusting shopping center. I would never write songs like that ever again.

And at that moment, as Wanker stood in the bitter cold, having a panic attack, he looked up as little icy diamonds of snow started to fall from the sky.

Guided by Demons debuted on the Billboard Charts at Number Two. The band embarks on a multi-city world tour this August.

Conjuring Danny Squires

There's a toy manufacturer named Hasbro. They're best known for making G.I. Joe, Rubik's Cube, and Baby Alive. Believe it or not, Hasbro has a direct communication line to the spiritual world. I'm talking about the Ouija board. Hasbro makes that, too. And for one summer we used it to talk to our friend Danny.

That July, all the yards in our subdivision were scorched brown by the relentless sun. The little parcels of grass in front of all the homes looked like beds of straw. The temperature was over ninety degrees for something like three weeks straight. The neighbor's dog, Nixon, a wirehair terrier, sat outside day after day, chained up, head hanging low, her hind leg occasionally twitching away a buzzing fly. When I think of the term, "the dog days of summer," I think of her, old Nixon. My little sister Maeve and I would regularly bring out a fresh bowl of water for her. Maeve even put ice cubes in it, but they melted right away.

One day, our friend Troy Gobel came over with a board game tucked under his arm. He was gangly, taller than most kids in the eighth grade, and he wore coke bottle glasses, the thickest you'd ever seen. Maeve and I were in the basement on the saggy couch, watching *The Munsters*. We didn't have air conditioning, and drank pitcherfuls of Kool-Aid that left electric blue stains above our upper lips.

"Hey, Troy."

"Check it out," he said. He sat down next to us on the brown plaid couch that once belonged to my grandma. We got it after she died. It still smelled like lavender and cigarettes.

Troy pulled out the box he was carrying.

OUIJA: Mystifying Oracle

"A new game!" Maeve kicked her feet up and down.

"You can use this to talk to the dead," said Troy.

"That don't work." I shook my head. "It's like the Magic 8 Ball."

"No, it's for real. Steve Swanson told me he once contacted Abraham Lincoln with it."

"What did Abe Lincoln say?" asked Maeve, bending her head and peering at the box top, obscuring most of it with her untamed beechwood blonde hair.

"The game board spelled out 'Ford,' and then they lost their connection. It's a bummer 'cause that would have been really cool."

"Steve Swanson is full of crap," I said.

"Whatever," Troy shot back. "You going to try it with me, or what?"

"Yeah!" said Maeve. "I hope we get someone good to talk to us."

"It needs to be dark down here," said Troy, looking around the basement. He stood up and walked to the bottom of the stairs and flipped the overhead fluorescent lights off. The only light source—the blazing dayglow of high summer—now came from three fishtank-sized basement windows set high in the walls.

"This is ridiculous," I said. "The dead don't talk to you."

"Just try it."

Troy sat down on the couch with us, and opened the box on the drink-stained, lacquered coffee table. He unfolded the game board. Printed on top was the alphabet—a gentle arc of letters A through Z, in a sort of spooky old

Victorian black type. Below that were numbers, one through ten. A pen and ink illustration of a black and white sun, replete with a smiling face, was in one corner; a sleepy crescent moon in the other. At the bottom of the board was the word "goodbye."

Troy scanned the directions on the inside of the box top. "Says here we have to put our hands on the 'planchette,'" Troy said.

We all three placed our hands on the heart-shaped plastic piece. In its center was a small, round clear window to view messages from the beyond. The planchette, with our hands on it, was supposed to move its way around the board, spelling out messages from the beyond.

Troy took a deep breath. Maeve watched him intently and did the same.

"We are trying to contact the spirit world," said Troy. "Can anyone hear us?"

The three of us sat still. We were so quiet, you could hear the pendulum inside the grandfather clock upstairs in the living room swinging away. Nixon barked.

Troy looked at me and nodded at the board, wanting me to ask the next question. When I didn't say anything, he glared. I rolled my eyes.

"Is anyone there?" Maeve asked.

Our fingertips rested lightly on the planchette.

"We would like to talk," said Maeve.

The thing started to move slightly. I looked up at Troy. He had his eyes closed. I knew he was moving it, the dork.

"Who's there?" asked Troy. "Who are we talking to?"

The plastic heart moved slowly across the board, over the arc of black lettering.

"Stop screwing around, Troy. You're moving this thing."

The piece stopped its questionably phantasmal glide.

"You broke our concentration!" said Troy. "We were connected to some-one!"

"Luke!" said Maeve, looking at me with disappointment. "Can't you just play along? Why do you have to be so serious all the time?"

"All right, all right," I said, taking a breath, lifting my fingers tips off the planchette a few inches and then placing them back down. I closed my eyes.

We sat in silence for a few seconds. Focusing.

"If there is a spirit here with us," said Troy, "please reveal yourself. You are amongst friends."

A few seconds passed and nothing. Then, effortlessly, like a plastic puck on an air-hockey table, it started gliding across the alphabet. It stopped on the letter "S." Then it moved again, drifting over to "Q."

It was bull. Troy or Maeve was moving the thing. I didn't believe it for one second. Still, a shiver came over me.

The planchette drifted across the board surface. It moved to "U," then "I," then "R," then "E," and finally to "S." Then it stopped.

S-Q-U-I-R-E-S

I looked at Troy. His eyes, even behind the thick prescription lenses, bulged. "Is that you, Danny?" asked Troy.

And the plastic heart began moving again. Y-E-S, it spelled.

Maeve sat up straight. "Oh, Danny," she whispered. "Are you really here? I miss you." She looked at me. "Luke, too."

~~~

Danny Squires used to live in our neighborhood. We went to school togeth-er, at Myrtle G. Schumacher Elementary. During the summers when our moms worked, we hung out every day. We were the kids of divorced parents, and we took care of ourselves. We watched TV. We made peanut butter and cheese sandwiches. We blasted KISS records in the basement. We read books, lots of them, and talked about them. One day, Danny came over with the first book in the *Hardy Boys'* detective series—*The Tower Treasure*—and we were hooked. We read a dozen or more books in the series after that. We hung out at the mall, went to the movies, and when that got boring, went to the forest preserve behind the mall and climbed trees like apes. Danny also took care of Maeve like she was his own sister. He played dolls with her when I wouldn't. He laughed at her nonsensical knock knock jokes.

"Knock knock?"

"Who's there?"

"Knock knock."

"Who's there!?"

"Knock knock!"

Danny always laughed at that one, going along with it. He used to say that he and Maeve were real brother and sister, since they had the same hair—untamed heads of stringy blonde.

One day, when we were walking along the railroad tracks that cut through town, he turned to me and said, "I love you, Luke."

Danny Squires is the only guy who ever said that to me. It wasn't weird or anything, just brotherly.

~~~

The first few months after he died, it didn't seem to really bother me. I think I was in a state of shock or denial. Then, one night lying in bed, I woke up, crying.

Drenched in sweat, I cried. Cold shafts of moonlight spotlighted in through my bedroom window. My hair was soaked. My Minnesota Viking pajamas were drenched. And I couldn't stop. Mom came into my room and sat on the edge of my bed.

"What's wrong, Luke?" she asked. She wrapped her arms around me and I tucked my head under her chin and I wept more.

"Why did Danny have to die?"

"I don't know, honey. I just don't know." She hugged me tighter.

We sat there a long time, her rocking me. Then I saw Maeve standing in the bedroom doorway, bathed in the white moonglow. She had on her favorite vanilla-colored flannel nightgown and she was holding her doll with the eyes that wouldn't shut.

"What's wrong?" she asked, in that high, pipsqueak voice of hers. "Luke, what's wrong? Don't cry."

"He's sad about Danny," Mom said.

"It's okay, Luke," Maeve said. "It's okay."

I sniffled as Mom held me tighter.

"Really, Luke," Maeve said again, looking at me very seriously. I'd never seen her like that. "It's okay."

~~~

Danny was gone over a year when we started playing with the Ouija board. We played it all the summer long. Each time, we supposedly connected to him. My nightmares started then. The car crash. The impact of the cars hitting; the tremendous jolting of mother and son. I could see the intersection, looking down on Carolyn Squires, after she had emerged from the mangled automobile, standing there in the cascading snowfall. Sometimes, in the twisted wreckage of the car, I could just make out a clump of Danny's blonde hair. I could smell the gasoline.

When I couldn't sleep any longer, Mom said maybe I should go see someone, but I didn't want to. I couldn't tell some therapist—some stranger—what I was feeling. We really didn't have the money for it anyway, so Mom dropped it.

Some nights I was afraid to go to bed. I was scared of falling asleep. The Ouija board wasn't helping anything. I didn't believe in it. But in the back of my mind, I thought that maybe, just maybe, we really were talking to Danny. So we sat down in the basement through the end of July and into August and asked him questions:

"Where are you?"

HEAVEN

"Are you happy there?

YES

"Would you come back if you could?"

NO

"Are there others there with you?"

YES

"Have you met anyone famous?

ELVIS IS HERE

I paused on this last one and looked up at Troy. He didn't meet my eyes; instead, he stared down at the game. This last response was pure crock. Troy's parents were obsessed with Elvis. When the King died, they drove to Graceland for the vigil. While they were there, they bought a bunch of Elvis plates with his face on it, an Elvis mirror, key-chains, T-shirts, coffee mugs, wristbands, pot holders, and loads of other crap. Their entire house was a shrine.

When the Ouija board spelled "Elvis is here," I knew that we weren't connected to Danny at all. It had been Troy all along.

"Screw you, Troy. You've been moving this thing yourself. We're not talking to Danny. It's you."

"I promise," said Troy, surprise on his face. "I haven't moved this thing once. Not once!"

"Come on, Troy. Just leave. And take the Ouija board with you. I've had enough."

"Whatever," Troy said, standing up. "If you don't believe me, fine. I'm telling you, I didn't fake any of this."

"Elvis, Troy?" I said, accusingly.

Maeve shrugged. "Elvis deserves to be in heaven," she said.

Troy walked up the basement stairs and left. We heard the front door slam behind him. He left the Ouija board. It sat there on the coffee table. Maeve and I sat in silence, staring at it. Then, the weirdest thing happened. The overhead fluorescent lights blinked on. All by themselves.

~~~

A week passed and we didn't touch the game. One afternoon, after the weather cooled off and there was an actual breeze blowing, Maeve and I walked home from the library. The sun shone through the rustling leaves in the trees along the streets, creating a sort of brilliant champagne-colored light. Everywhere there was the constant buzz of cicadas. Before we went inside, Maeve filled Nixon's water dish. When we went down to the basement. The TV was on.

"That's weird," I said. "I'm sure I turned the TV off."

Then I noticed a book lying on the floor. A *Hardy Boys* book had fallen off a shelf. I picked it up and looked at it. *The Tower Treasure*.

"See?" said Maeve. "Danny is here. The TV was turned on. A book flew off a shelf. That's the sort of thing ghosts do."

It's hard to tell the difference sometimes, when something you really want to be real *is* real, or if you just want it so badly to be real that you convince yourself of it.

"It's nothing," I said, finally. "Just a weird coincidence."

"Come on," said Maeve, moving over to the Ouija board. "Let's see."

I stood there for a moment. I was tired of it. Mostly of the nightmares. But, always in the back of my mind, what if? What if that darned board game was a conduit to Danny? So I went and sat next to Maeve and placed my hands next to hers on the plastic planchette.

"Danny," Maeve said. "Are you here with us?"

The planchette began moving. Drifting, drifting, with a little more momentum than usual. My eyes met Maeve's. The device moved over the letters, finally spelling: I AM WITH YOU.

Maeve smiled at me. A sweet, innocent smile.

"Did you do that? Did you move it to say that?" I asked, urgently.

Maeve looked at me for a moment before answering, firmly, "No."

~~~

Danny never really knew his dad. He was an only child and his mom worshipped him. He was her everything. Carolyn Squires had a bleached bouffant hairdo and she listened to a lot of sad country music about heartbreak and death and stuff. Most of the time I was over at Danny's house, she was seated on the floral sofa reading the Bible. She was a secretary at a local factory. One night in the dead of winter, Mrs. Squires was driving her powder blue Mercury Marquis—the same exact color as the eye shadow she always wore—from the Ridgedale Mall. Danny sat in the passenger seat. Mrs. Squires had just bought Danny some soft corduroys and oxford shirts for school. They were talking about going away on summer vacation together, to California. Mrs. Squires had both of her hands on the wheel, her red nails clenching the cold molded plastic. It had snowed most of the day. One of the headlights on the car was out. Mrs.

Squires said she was going to fix it with her next paycheck. Patches of black ice were everywhere.

The car moved through an intersection and then there was a great explosion of metal and glass, like a bomb going off. The other car had missed the red light and hit the passenger side of the Squires' car. The impact was tremendous. Inside, particles of burnt tobacco floated slowly in the air—thrown from the ashtray. Glass showered the floor, papers from the glove box floated. Mrs. Squires clenched the wheel tightly with her hands and gritted her teeth. After the violent collision, everything became still. She looked over at her son. That side of the car had been destroyed completely. Imploded.

Shaking, muttering, "no ... no ... no ... ," she unbuckled herself and stepped from the vehicle out into the cold night and barren intersection. The other car was accordioned. The lone driver slumped over the steering wheel. Steam hissed from what was left of the car's radiator. Carolyn Squires stood there, underneath the bright corner streets lamps as snow flittered down. Her son was dead.

~~~

That night, after Mom got home from work, I asked her to drive me to the Ridgedale Mall. She and Maeve went shopping and I took the escalator up to the second level to the Game Kingdom—a small emporium of board games, model kits, toy soldiers, and trading cards. The owner, a man with a big belly wearing a baseball cap to cover a balding hairline, was seated behind a glass counter.

"What's up, boss?" he asked, turning the volume down on a small portable television he was watching. There was a sit-com on, and I could still hear the occasional wave of canned studio laughter.

"Do you sell Ouija boards?"

"Sure do. There, over on that shelf." He pointed to the corner of the shop.

72

"I actually have one already, I was hoping you might be able to answer some questions for me."

"Sure, I'll do the best I can. What's up?"

"Is a Ouija board real?" I asked. "I mean, does it really help communicate to the spirit world?"

"Depends what your definition of 'real' is. Are the Vikings going to be real this year? I suppose. If you believe. If you want to believe."

"What can you tell me about the rules of playing the game?"

The owner lifted the brim of his cap and scratched his forehead. "Well, there are a couple of rules and points you need to follow. Lots of people take Ouija boards very seriously. They say that if you don't do things right, you could set loose a spirit and keep it trapped here on our plane of existence. Spirits don't want to be here. Seriously, man. It sucks. You think a ghost wants to contend with our earthly problems? And if they are stuck here, they can't rest in peace. Worse yet, some people maintain that if you really screw things up with a Ouija board, you can inadvertently set *demons* free. Believe me, you don't want that. There was one kid in Minnetonka I heard about who released Asmodeus by accident."

"What happened?"

"It was a bad scene. Asmodeus evidently got into the plumbing system of the house because he was attracted to the stench. It ended up costing the parents like ten grand to replace the septic tank. Brutal."

"Did they get rid of the demon?"

"Beats me."

"Well how do you screw things up with a Ouija board?"

"You got to follow the rules. At the bottom of the game board, there's the word 'goodbye.' When you're done communicating with a spirit, you need to end the session by bidding it farewell. The spirit will move the floating plastic thing down and spell out 'goodbye.' This makes sure that any ghost, demon, or spirit returns to their own plane of existence."

"What happens if you end a game and forget to do this?"

"I'm not sure. You might have a spirit with you for the rest of your life. I suppose you can always try to go back, play again, and this time say goodbye for good. At some point you just need to let the spirit go home."

"Is there anything else important when playing a Ouija board?"

"Well, they say you have to play with more than one person. But I think that's a load of shit. Think about it, man. If a ghost is in your house, it's going to do whatever the hell it wants. It doesn't need two people with their hands on a plastic part made by Hasbro. A ghost could just move that thing. I mean, come on! The real reason they want you to play with more than one person is so one person can cheat and move that piece across the board and the other person will just wonder if it moved for real. That's why."

I wondered again if Troy or Maeve had been moving the thing all along.

"And sometimes," the owner continued, "people don't even know they're moving it themselves. It's a subconscious deal."

"You can move the game piece and not even know you are doing it?"

"Sometimes."

"Oh," I said, surprised. "Well, thanks for all your help."

"Anytime, boss."

I turned to leave. The owner turned the volume up on his television and I heard the eruption of studio audience laughter. I went out into the mall, leaned over the second-tier railing, and spotted my Mom and Maeve, sitting down in the lower level food court. You couldn't miss Maeve—she loved to wear this cute red beret. They were having ice cream. I took the escalator downstairs and met up with them.

We drove home. After they went to bed, I went down to the basement. I watched Johnny Carson for a while—something Danny and I used to do when he spent the night. When everything was quiet upstairs, I turned the TV off, dimmed the lights and lit two white dinner candles Mom kept in a drawer. I took a seat on the couch. The Ouija board was spread out before me. I took a deep breath, closed my eyes, and placed my hands on the planchette. I sat silently for a minute. It was so quiet, I could hear the pulse in my head.

"Danny, if you are here, let me know. Give me a sign."

I waited. The room glowed from the candlelight. Next door, out in the night, I heard Nixon bark.

"I miss you, Danny," I said. "If you're here with me please give me a sign."

I waited, my fingers placed gently on the planchette. It didn't move. Nixon barked again.

"I can't stop the nightmares, Danny. The bad dreams of your accident. They won't go away."

My eyes welled with warm, salty tears.

"Danny, I just want to know. I want to know if—"

The planchette began to move, just skimming above the game board. I was a little startled. I even took my fingers off of it for a second and I swear to you, even looking back on it now, it moved all on its own. I rested my fingertips back on the plastic pointer. It moved quickly across the board, with urgency. And I watched as it spelled it out. Spelled right before my eyes.

IT'S OK

And with my fingers resting gently on the planchette, I did what I was supposed to do along, what any responsible Ouija player does, I said goodbye to Danny Squires. When I was through, I closed the board game, put it away in the box, and blew the candles out. I ascended the stairs in darkness, went to my bedroom, climbed into bed, and for the first time in a long time, fell into a deep and restful sleep.

Monsters and Angels

The night blew in the tall prairie grasses. In the distance, he could see the silhouette of a small log cabin, alone, out there. As he sat atop his horse on a hill of grass, it seemed as if all the stars were in slight motion, circling, circling, the nearly imperceptible rotation of the cosmos. He could hear the chorus of crickets, the distant cry of a wolf, the whipping wind, and, if he listened closely, *really listened*, the gentle hum of the universe itself.

He rode closer to the cabin. It was long abandoned. The front door was open, creaking back and forth in the warm night wind. There were glass windows, the panes jagged and broken. They would need replacing.

He had traveled far. Across Ohio, Indiana, Illinois, Iowa, and now, here in Nebraska, he decided he had traveled far enough. The abandoned cabin might be a good place to stop. To begin to rebuild his life, or what was left of it. If he could even rebuild it at all. How many miles had he run? How far had he gone trying to leave his troubles? It was all still there, of course, in his head, his heart, and in the pit of his stomach. He wished it would all just go away.

He dismounted his dusty horse and unpacked what little he had brought with him. He was dusty himself. He wiped the sweat above his eyes and rubbed his sun-hardened hands through his coarse, gray beard.

Inside, he lit a tin barn lantern, tiny holes punched in the metal. He took stock of the single room cabin. It was mostly empty, save for an overturned wooden chair and table. Shards of china were scattered on the floor and, odd, a tarnished silver baby rattle lay in the corner. People built cabins out in the prairie, he thought, and then, for various reasons, abandoned them, moved on. They left to move farther west, looking for new opportunities, reuniting with distant family—or, they had grown weary of the desolation of a place like the Great Plains.

The roof of the cabin seemed in good shape, no holes for the rain to come in, none that he could see, at least, from the flickering lantern light.

He unrolled his wool blanket, took his Stetson off and his worn leather boots, lowered his suspenders, and fell asleep on the floor.

~~~

The same dream: The Cincinnati tavern. The man with the red jowls and the high octave voice.

"A preacher ain't supposed to be patronizing an establishment of this kind," the voice echoes. "Shame on you, sir!"

As always, he ignores the man. Or he tries.

The man gets closer. Draws in. He can smell his sweat. He can feel the furnace of alcohol on his breath.

"Proverbs tells us," the man says, "'Be not among drunkards or among gluttons, for the drunkard and the glutton will come to poverty, and slumber will clothe them with rags.' A preacher should know such things."

He turns to the man and steadies his voice.

"Take heed of your own advice, traveler. Please, leave me alone."

~~~

He woke at daybreak. The horizon was split by pinks and oranges and above it blue and then cobalt and one last remaining morning star, fading.

He stepped from the cabin.

The grasslands went on around him, in every direction, to the horizon. The land was rolling and moving in the wind and endless as the sea.

He fed his horse some grain and shared what little water he had left with her. He set out on foot to survey the land around the cabin and discovered, just a short distance away, a few untidy rows of vegetables, some squashes and onion and cabbage plants that had been hit by insects. The plants climbed upward, their leaves wild.

As he surveyed further, he was grateful to find a well dug deep into the dry earth. And there was water at the bottom. Whoever had inhabited the log cabin had done good work on it. To make it right.

He spent the morning on horseback, exploring. The wind blew the mixed grass fields in waves: switchgrass, bluestem, and constellations of wildflowers.

After an hour of riding, kept company by grackles and butterflies and the occasional black-tailed prairie dog lifting its curious head in his direction, he spotted a row of trees on the horizon, a sure sign of a creek or a river. As he approached, indeed, the land slanted down to a creek bottom, slow flowing. He let his horse drink and wade in the cool water. It was getting hot and he was about done.

He pictured his son, Jeremy, eight years old, born after the war. He laughed often, his eyes squinting as he did so. He lived to make others laugh.

Some days after his eighth birthday, Jeremy caught a cold and it went to his lungs. He was born two months early, his breathing always labored when he ran, when he was sick. Every day for weeks, he coughed and coughed and his gray eyes, like his father's, welled with tears from the strain. They boiled water so he could breathe the steam, but it brought him little relief. And as the nights carried on, he would fall asleep for slivers of rest and, one morning, he did not wake.

Mother was the first to check on him. She screamed for father. Their son's face was a slight shade of blue, the very same shade as the dim light of the pre-dawn hours. He ran for help and men arrived from the hospital and took his son's body away that dawn.

He turned to the Bible, of course, as he always instructed his parishioners to do. He tried his best to hand his sorrow to the Lord. But quietly, secretly, he turned to drinking, during the day and especially at night. It made it better, it gave him some courage, it lessened the pain, but when the effects wore off, it made things worse.

And then there was the tavern and the man who would not leave him alone.

~~~

Prairie hens. Ring-necked pheasant. White-tailed deer. The vegetable garden—there was plenty of food. One afternoon, he spotted a lone figure on horseback on the horizon. The silhouette drew larger as it approached the cabin. It was a man, tall and bearded, wearing a Stetson. He dismounted his horse and approached him with a nod and a firm handshake. He brought a fresh baked loaf of bread. He said he lived about ten miles away, in a cabin of his own, on the other side of the creek bottoms. He introduced himself as Seamus Walsh.

He explained that the nearest town, Kearney, was about 40 miles away. He lived alone. They talked a while. Mr. Walsh said he could share seeds and plantings from his own farm, to help repair anything with the cabin.

They considered the window panes. He would need to go to town, soon, to replace them and to stock up on provisions before the weather shifted towards autumn. It was good to have such a neighbor. Sometimes when you are hurting, he thought, the company of a good person can quell the pain, if only for a time.

"Who built this cabin?" he asked Mr. Walsh.

"A young couple. Very quiet. They had a baby. But the child was never well.

I helped them dig the well you found out back. It was a hard job, but it helped them."

"What happened to them?"

"The poor child didn't even make it to her first birthday. She died and the mother and father were never the same. I came around now and again, but they both suffered. The worst I have ever encountered."

"The baby," he asked. "Do you know what was wrong with her?"

Seamus Walsh looked out at the land. "The child was never healthy, never destined to live long. I don't know what the trouble was. But the parents lost their patience with her. I saw it with my own eyes. They didn't have the means to care for her. I fear the fate of that child may have been grim, and she died unjustly."

"How do you know this for certain?"

"I don't. It's just a strong feeling."

The two men were quiet for a time.

"Those folks left some months after the baby died. Just moved on. Never said goodbye. They took nothing with them. The cabin was looted after that. What you found was all that was left."

"I cannot believe they would harm their child," he said. "I had a son. I loved him."

After he said this, his eyes pooled with tears and Seamus Walsh moved close and put his arm around him and reminded him of God's word.

"We fix our eyes not on what is seen," he said, "but on what is unseen, since what is seen is temporary, but what is unseen is eternal ..."

"Thank you," he said. "Kind of you."

~~~

The man followed him out of the tavern. Around a corner. He ducked down a dark alley, the pavement wet with puddles from a fresh rain. It smelled of horse manure and of scraps of raw meat tossed from a nearby butcher shop. He turned. The man with the ruddy face was behind him, walking slowly and determinedly down the brick alleyway, stepping in the puddles and muddying his boots and trousers and the bottom of his long jacket.

"I want no trouble, sir!" he said.

"You are a sinful man," the follower said, pointing at him, "yet you preach the word of the Lord! Have you no shame?"

He stopped as the man approached, his belly and arms heavy with rolls of flesh. Their faces were now inches apart.

"I said, let me be," he said in a low, whispered register. "You don't know what I have been through, sir. As I know not your pain."

The man was sweating, heaving.

"Hypocrite."

"Don't antagonize me."

The man pushed his shoulder, hard. He stumbled back a few steps.

"Don't do this."

"I don't like you."

"I don't like what you're doing."

The man swung his fist, his knuckles white, connecting with his jaw.

After the war, after its violence, the blood, the dying, he had lost his will to fight. But the man would not stop. So, he swung back, connecting with the man's nose. Blood gushed out of both nostrils, pooled in his whiskers.

The man withdrew a bowie knife from a sheath hidden under his coat. The iron blade glinted in the darkness of the alleyway. The man stepped forward and swung. He had not encountered violence of this nature since the wooded hills of Chicamauga.

He grabbed the man's arm, corded with more anger and muscle than he'd expected, the knife raised high above them both. He felt it then. Anger. It welled up. He had no thought, other than that.

They jostled in the alley, taking steps back and forth. He was younger than this man, he was faster, and he was stronger. He yanked the knife from the man's grip and, without explanation, without thought, plunged it squarely into his stomach. It was so easy, the abdomen soft and loamy. The man fish-eyed. Warm blood flowed onto his hand. It felt good to strike at something.

The man vomited. A figure at the end of the alleyway stopped and looked in their direction.

"Stop!"

He pulled the knife from the man's stomach, like a butcher easily slicing flesh. Bright blood spurted from the man's stomach. He collapsed.

What have I done? Dear Lord.

The man lay on the wet, dirty brick coughing up bile.

A second story window on the back of a building opened. A woman's voice cried out in the night, "What have you done to him?!"

He dropped the bloody knife, and it clanged on the bricks. The man on the ground closed his eyes. His breathing slowed.

He turned and ran. Another voice in the night yelled, "Stop! Stop!"

He ran and he ran.

~~~

Autumn swept across the prairie. The land browned into a palette of straw and ochre. The late summer cicadas had shriveled and died, their evening nocturne silenced.

The October sun shifted cold. He traveled to Kearney and replaced the glass in the windows. The fireplace in the cabin was clean and ready for the hard winter months ahead. Mr. Walsh had visited several times, helping him, keeping him company. One morning, they sat outside on a wooden bench he built, drank coffee, and talked.

"Why do you live out here, Seamus? Alone?"

"We all seek desolation at times, I suppose. To escape the pain of the past, or the noise of the present, or the uncertainty of the future. I saw things in the war, I did things. I never want to repeat them."

He looked out at the fields and the meadowlarks darting about.

"I killed a man," he said, after a long silence.

"In the war?" Seamus asked.

"No. Not then. Outside a tavern. After Jeremy died. I don't know what overcame me. A fever. The devil. People saw me. A policeman. I am certain I am a wanted man," he stopped and drank his coffee. Finally, he continued. "I was certain I would never speak of it. I left my wife. I abandoned her. I left everything. I have lost everything."

A yellow-tufted meadowlark landed nearby. Seamus placed his hand on his shoulder.

"I believe you can run for eternity, you know, and not go anywhere."

~~~

Winter descended on the prairie like a gray wave crashing upon the shore and it did not recede for months. He hunted. He built fires. Mr. Walsh visited. He read his Bible.

In the early weeks of December, the first snowfall had powdered the grass fields and the sun had all but gone into hibernation. He would lie in his bed at night and listen to the snarling wind beyond the walls. With each night, it seemed to grow fiercer. It howled. A haunting wail like a train furnacing in the night.

One night, he arose from his bed. Awakened by the sound, he peered out the small rectangular window. The white silver snow was swirling, rising up in cyclones. It moved, out there on the plains. As he watched, they almost looked alive, these snow devils, contorting, spinning, churning, tearing up frozen earth. Sometimes the might of nature stunned him.

Several nights later, again, the howling wind summoned him from bed. And he awoke and peered out the lead glass and the cyclones of snow were shapeshifting in the white beyond. He squinted, looking out upon these dervishes, and suddenly one of the cyclones seemed to sprout wings from its twisting torso. The wings fanned out and upward, like angel wings or, perhaps, the webbed sails of a demon. The cyclone moved, the snow wings flapping.

One night in January, he counted six snow cyclones beyond the cabin, howling, great wings of snow, trying to take flight. At one point, heads emerged, beaked like tremendous birds, wings of white gusting. They looked like phoenixes or maddened snow dragons; monsters or angels, he could not decide.

One of the great snow beasts cycloned closer to the cabin. The little house shook. He stood at the window, crouched down as it twisted closer. It spun up next to the cabin, its great wings fanning skyward, the point of one needled the window and shattered the pane, sending glass shards at his face. His face bloodied from dozens of tiny cuts, spidering his cheeks.

~~~

Mild days came. An early thaw. Seamus Walsh rode up to the cabin one morning. They had coffee. They talked about plans for their land come spring. Before Mr. Walsh left, he stopped him.

"Seamus," he said. "I have visitors at night. From the snow."

Mr. Walsh rubbed his wind-whipped cheeks.

"I'm not sure what you speak of."

"Out on the prairie. Snowbirds. Snow devils or snow angels. Perhaps both?

I see them often. Monsters and angels. They have wings and seem ... somehow ... alive."

Mr. Walsh paused before speaking.

"What is it?" he asked.

"The couple who lived here before you, the winter after their child died, they told me they saw the very same things. Creatures of snow. I told the husband—winter on the great plains, the isolation, it can play tricks on the mind." Seamus Walsh looked up and out upon the land. "He had seen them ... out there."

"What did you say? Did you believe him?"

"I didn't tell him, but I have seen them, too."

"Have you?"

"Once. I refused to believe my eyes. But the husband. He insisted they were quite real. I'll never forget what he said."

"What did he say, Seamus?"

"He said, 'The snow creatures, they are here, gathering outside my cabin either to redeem me or condemn me, I don't know which, God or Devil.'"

~~~

The dream was different. He was in a city cemetery. The headstones were already faded, darkened.

The casket was being lowered into the frozen earth. The body of the man he had killed was inside, locked beneath the lid. Standing nearby, around the great hole in the earth, were many mourners, in black, watching the scene. He saw in his dream a wife and a young child, both sobbing.

He was there, off to the side, watching.

~~~

He awoke, long after midnight, to the sound of the wind. It was shrill and melodious, at once a chorus, then, a bottomless pit of screams. The sound was louder and more intense than ever. At first, he thought he would stay under the quilt. They were out there, he knew—the dervishes. Perhaps he could just ignore them. But the wailing crescendoed. And then the other window, the one not boarded up, shattered, glass bulleting in and raining to the floor.

With resolve, he put on his shirt, his trousers, his suspenders, his wool socks, and his boots.

Crystals of dark snow came in through the broken window. He looked out into the night. There were three of them. Three tremendous snow birds, wings out, soaring on the prairie with great force. The snow beasts wailed in the night.

He walked to the door, took his heavy wool coat from a hook, grabbed his hat, and lowered it down near his eyes.

He opened the door, letting in the cold universe beyond. And he stepped out. The three snow cyclones twisted and moved and churned frozen earth, clawing it up with ease. He closed the cabin door behind him and walked out into the night, out onto the prairie towards the monsters or the angels. He kept walking until all three spun towards him, enveloping him, completely, in white.

All the Summer Before Us

Back in those days, we could still make out the stars in the night sky, all the pinpoints of light along with the constellations—Orion, Cassiopeia, Ursa Major and Minor.

We were surrounded on all sides by cornfields rustling in the early summer air. Those night green fields went on and on. At least it seemed that way. There was a remarkable lack of ambient light back then, in this stretch of western Illinois. This was before the incessant creep of asphalt and Klieg lights and big box stores—before the rural acquiesced to suburban sprawl.

We were eighteen, me and Dave and Bill; childhood friends on the cusp of adulthood. On a silent country road we had discovered an old concrete pipe factory out amidst the darkness and the corn stalks that would, in weeks, be knee-high by the fourth of July.

We parked our car in a subdivision about a mile away from the factory. This was the first subdivision of many that would soon arrive, a harbinger of the development to come, a real estate malignancy bearing such ironic monikers as "Cedar Ridge" and "Willow Creek." We were in Dave's nocturnal blue Chevy with scrunched-up fast food bags on the floor and heavy metal looping from the glowing stereo. Dave killed the headlights. We rolled up the windows and stepped from the car. It was a Midwest summer night: crickets in the fields a June night chorus. A firefly rose from the ground, drifting spirit light. A freight train off somewhere in the distance passed.

As we walked, the concrete factory loomed, a shadowy industrial acropolis with a rising sheet metal tower and a connected rundown warehouse. An old chain link fence surrounded the place. We found an opening and sneaked in. Hundreds of concrete pipes of various sizes were stacked up like toys in the vast gravel yard. They were drainage pipes, many of them large enough to stand inside. What called us to this place, we did not know. But we were drawn to it nonetheless. We wandered around the gravel lot, through the labyrinthine corridors of stacked concrete pipes.

Everything about the factory building was covered in rust. The tower, some sort of silo we assumed for mixing cement, had a rusted ladder attached and we decided to climb.

The ladder felt precarious, going up at least four stories. Yet, undaunted and for no apparent reason, we continued to ascend. As we got higher and higher the view was magnificent. We reached the roof of the tower and looked out at the dark cornfields rustling in tremendous sheets in the summer night. Far off, we could see the lights of Sterling Springs.

We stepped upon the roof of the old factory. We talked, three young men who were, really, three boys. We lay down on the roof and stared up at the stars and we pondered where our lives would take us. What we didn't realize then is that none of that really mattered. What mattered then, was that moment, and our friendship, and the very fact that all the world was out before us.

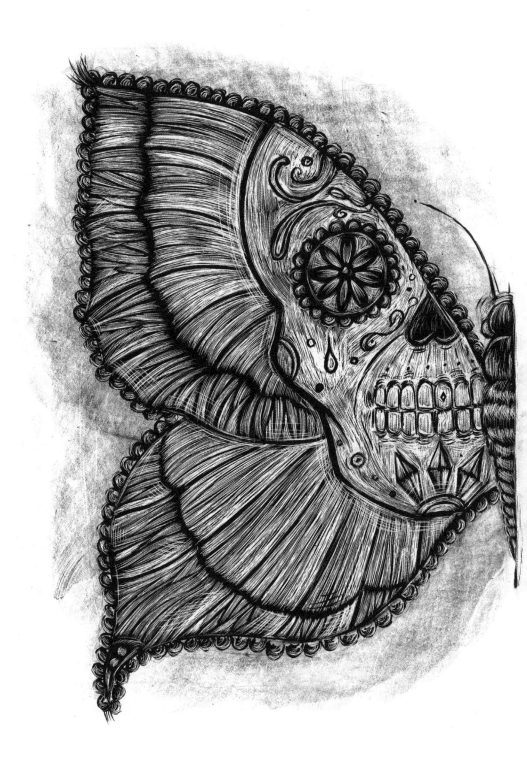

The Girl in the Funeral Parlor

When I was twenty, I got a job delivering flowers. Three days a week, I drove a Chevy van, the words "Forget Me Not" painted on the sides, down barren two-lane western Illinois county roads.

There was a solitude to the job that I liked. As soon as the van was loaded and I drove away from the flower shop, no one could tell me what to do. Sometimes, on busy days, I would be gone for three, four hours, maybe longer. Talk radio and a supersized soda kept me company, and I just lived in my head.

I delivered to offices all over town for all their celebrations—every week someone threw a party on ersatz holidays like Sweetest Day (do we seriously need a Sweetest Day when we have Valentine's Day?). Then there were Saturday mornings at churches, where weddings were set up; Saturday afternoons included dropping off arrangements for the following day's services.

I also delivered to rickety bungalows in our small city, brick apartment buildings in the center square, and lonesome houses miles outside town. In winter, when it's dark early and ghosts of snow blow across the rural highways, it's always a little eerie. After driving down a gravel road to some farm, I'd have to step out into the sub-zero wind chill and approach the dark house. Sometimes, a dog would bark and scratch at the door after I knocked. I'd wait a minute or two, hoping no one was home. Then I could just leave. But then, a light would blink on. I'd hear heavy footsteps; several dead bolts, one after another, being undone, and then the door would open a sliver. A pale face would peer out.

"Yes?"

"Flower delivery!"

In those moments, out there in the stubbly frozen hinterland, facing some stranger in shadow, I shivered, wondering if I would ever be seen again.

Without a doubt, though, I found delivering to funeral parlors the weirdest of all. My job was to lay the flowers around the casket. Averting my eyes and crouching, I'd set up the floral sprays and plants quickly around the body. Sometimes, with a casket spray arrangement, I would actually have to place it on the closed bottom half of the coffin.

It felt odd being there, alone with the dead. Here I was, a community-college kid studying English Lit and living with his parents, arranging flowers over the mortal remains of the dearly departed. They never knew me while they lived, and I felt like I was violating them in a way. It just felt perverted.

On one of these occasions, at the old Peterson Funeral Home, I encountered Catherine Courington. She was dead, yet more alive than anyone I'd ever known.

It was an early June morning, when sunlight splashed through oak leaves over the funeral home, casting a glow. The van was packed from end-to-end and perfumed with fountains of crimson roses, white lilies, and waxen orchids. The labels on some of the flowers were marked:

Peterson Funeral Home – Courington Service

The Peterson family ran that funeral home in town for over a hundred years, in a Victorian built on top of a hill leading down to the Rock River. I liked the house's lead glass windows, thick and wide, and covered with gauzy lace curtains that sometimes shifted in the hot summer breeze. A cupola topped the three-story house and a winding red-brick walkway led up to a wraparound porch, where sometimes I'd see people dressed in black, stand and stare. In their sorrow, they probably didn't notice much. The hanging geranium baskets above them twisted in the breeze.

I parked the van behind the house. The old mansion had a back door, reserved for deliveries. I think this was where they brought in the bodies, to prepare them for the services, but I wasn't sure. An antiseptic, sterile odor I imagined was cleaning supplies and embalming fluid hung in the air.

With a bulky arrangement cradled in my arms, I walked to the back door. It was opened a crack, so I pushed it wide with my foot. After calling out and no one answering, I stepped into the darkened back hall and waited for my eyes to adjust. Somewhere in the house, a mantle clock ticked. No one was downstairs, but that's the way it was a few hours before a service. I pictured the funeral home people in their administrative offices on the uppermost floor, hurriedly finishing last details upstairs.

The parlor I found up front was long, enough to hold the casket and velvety sofas. The papered walls had a textured, moss green, fleur-de-lis pattern. Paintings of rivers, prairies, and meadows hung on the walls. Over the fireplace was the main painting, a crusty framed oil of William Peterson, the first of the family to settle here. He looked stern; his cravat stiff under his chin. I supposed the room looked exactly as it did when old William started the place. It sort of freaked me out, being alone in that parlor. It was just me and the body in the casket. It was open for viewing. Old William watched me. I laid the floral arrangement below the casket.

Something caught my eye; a flash, and quickly gone. I don't know why I looked that day over to the top of the casket. I thought maybe it was a shimmer of sunlight, over that area.

I stood and stared at the person in the casket. Jesus. She was young—she looked my age, maybe a little older. She wore a cardigan sweater, soft-looking and lilac, and a single strand of pearls. Her face had the slight bloating of the deceased, but it was smooth. Her eyes were lined in black with little points at the edges; her lips glossed in dark red; her hands folded across her chest. The top of a black-and-white polka dot skirt was visible. You couldn't see her legs. She looked like she had lived in the Fifties. And she looked peaceful. I know they say that about dead people, but I felt peace about her, a quietness that was reassuring. The more I looked, the more I felt that way. I felt an odd urge to touch that soft sweater. I glanced over my shoulder.

I didn't, or couldn't, do it. I looked down at her face. I wanted her eyes to open. I wanted her to speak. I wished it. I really wished it. *Just say something.*

After a long while, or maybe it was just a minute, I shook my head to clear it. Then I went back out into the sunlight to grab the other flowers. After setting up the rest of the arrangements, I looked at a sympathy card on one delivery: Catherine Courington.

I stared at her one last time. And without further thought, I ran my fingertips down the sleeve on her arm, and it was as petal soft and fuzzy as I'd imagined.

I turned and left.

~~~

Every day that next week, I thought about Catherine. I wondered how she died. How she lived. What she liked to read. Sometimes, when I was driving down roads, passing an occasional car headed in the opposite direction, I imagined that we had run into each other, that we became fast friends, and that we fell in love. I could see it. I felt this connection that I couldn't explain.

One night, I dreamed that we were at an outdoor café. A cathedral bell tolled in the far distance. We set our white coffee cups on the wrought-iron table. It felt so peaceful. She smiled. She was about to say something.

But I woke before she said a word.

In another dream she emerged from darkness, like she was in a warehouse without a single window or light source. She walked forward slowly, her hair buoyant on her shoulders, almost a halo around her. Her eyes were lined with that black eyeliner with the sharp points at the edges. She lifted her hand. My heart leapt.

I'm listening.

As she drew near, her face began to melt, like a wax figure in a Saturday horror matinee. Her make-up ran down her face in streams of colors. The rest of her face started dripping, her eyes and nose and lips. The molten wax swirled, morphing. As it began to take shape, I knew what it was. It was one of those Mexican Day of the Dead masks—a white skull painted boldly black, red, blue, and yellow, with white flowers.

She opened her mouth.

I'm listening.

But something emerged from her mouth other than words. It was dark, at first, small and twitching. As it crawled forth it showed itself. Wings. Black and orange. A butterfly fluttered and flew off into the darkness.

I woke, sweating and heart thumping. I swear I could still see her.

After these dreams, I had to know what had happened to her.

One late night, I searched the Internet. I didn't know why I hadn't before. I guess I felt weird about it, like it was perverted. I knew it was bizarre. I knew no one would understand, so I never said anything about it.

I sat in my room in the basement of my parents' house, in front of my computer and typed in her name. So many social networking pages of people named Catherine Courington popped up. I scrolled through each page, hoping to find a photo, to see her. I was really hoping for a video, to hear her. After hours, I found nothing. She didn't have a social network page.

I did find an unknown English poet with the same name—Catherine Courington, killed in a horse-and-carriage accident in 1882. She had died before any literary success.

I read a line of one of her poems: *The Clock Ticks Unfair ...*

Then a last page and I found her. I clicked on the link and the page began to load. It was just a small obituary item:

> *Catherine Courington, 21, of New York City.*
> *Beloved Daughter of Candace* (née Roberts)
> Funeral services, Saturday, June 10, 11 AM,
> *Peterson Funeral Home*, 111 S. Main Street.

~~~

The next day, I delivered flowers in a hurry, moving across town more like a FedEx guy than a flower man. I needed to buy myself an hour so my employers wouldn't ask where I was.

After looking up the information on Catherine Courington's mother, I discovered that she lived in a mobile home park, off a winding highway. I drove out after lunch.

The Fountain Bleu Mobile Home Park sign was faded, and paint was chipping off the bottom. As I pulled in, a kid ran across the street, chasing a ball. I slammed on the brakes, the van lurching, barely missing him. He was so close I could see his crew cut was very short and his face had plenty of freckles. He glared at me.

"Sorry," I mouthed and waved. In the sideview mirror, I could see him as I pulled the van forward, standing with his ball, scowling.

The mobile homes of Fountain Bleu were so run down that they looked like haunted trailers, with plywood planking and stained bedsheets over the windows. But a few had flower gardens and new shiny mailboxes in front. I found Candace Courington's mobile home at the end of the street. A Doberman chained to the neighboring house barked, baring its teeth. A man working over the engine of an El Camino looked up at me. I nodded. He didn't say a word, or nod back. He wiped sweat from his brow.

Plastic flowers spun in the wind along the sidewalk to the mobile home. The windows had metal horizontal blinds turned shut. I stepped up to the door and knocked. The guy across the street wiped his oily hands on a towel and watched me. The dog continued to bark, straining against its leash.

The door opened just a bit.

The woman held a lit cigarette in her hand. She had a dome of swimming pool blonde hair and tired eyes.

"Can I help you?" she asked.

"Candace Courington?"

"Yes," she said, looking over my shoulder to the van parked on the street.

"Flower delivery," I said, extending the arrangement in my arms.

She took it.

"Thanks." Her cigarette dangled from her lips. She began to close the door.

"I knew your daughter," I blurted, my words running together, before she could shut the door.

"Oh yeah?"

"I'm so sorry."

"Thanks," she said. "How did you know her?"

"High school." I thought about Sir Walter Scott's old quote about webs and lies.

"You went to school in New York?" she asked. "What are you doing out here, in Sterling Springs?"

"This is actually where I grew up. My parents just moved there for a few years and that's how I met Catherine."

I had no clue where this was going.

99

"That so," she said.

"The flowers are from me." I tried a smile.

Candace Courington looked at the arrangement. "That's nice of you."

She stepped back to close the door. I knew this was my only chance. "Can I tell you a story about Catherine, Mrs. Courington? A story from our days in New York?"

Jesus.

She stared at me for a moment, thoughtfully.

"Sure," she said, at last. "Come in. You want a glass of water?"

"If you don't mind."

The living room was dimly lit, and piles of bills were stacked on end tables, alongside prescription pill bottles.

We sat on a saggy sofa, with the plaid cloth worn thin on the edges. There was a framed print of that Impressionist painting by Seurat, "Sunday in the Park," or whatever it's called. It's weird that all the people in that painting, all the women with their parasols, the men with their top hats and the dogs and the kids, and even the monkey, are all facing the lake or away. But not the little girl. That kid with her white dress and bonnet, right in the middle of the painting, is looking right at you. Through your soul.

Candace Courington went to get me a glass of water from the kitchen. On a coffee table was a magazine, *Modern Amputee*. I picked it up and looked at the blonde woman posing on the cover. She wore a prosthetic leg.

I thumbed through some unopened envelopes next to the magazine. There was one, addressed to Catherine Courington, 210 E. 5th Street, New York, New York, that was a phone bill. I folded it and put it my back pocket. I felt like a douche bag, but kept it anyway.

"What's your name?" asked Candace Courington, returning to the room and handing me the glass of water.

"I'm Josh. Josh Dieboldt."

"What do you do, Josh? Besides deliver flowers, I mean?" She sat down next to me. We were both sunk so low, it felt like we were sitting on the floor.

"I'm studying English Lit at Rock River College."

"What do you want to do with that?"

"Be a writer, maybe." I shrugged and picked up the water glass but didn't drink it.

Candace Courington stared at the brown carpeting. "Catherine was a reader. She always had a book in her hands. Ever since she was little."

She looked up.

"So what story were you going to tell me? How did you two meet?"

Across the street, a car engine growled—a six-cylinder Godzilla. The guy in the driveway had started his El Camino.

"We just met on the street one afternoon. May," I said. "It smelled like flowers and garbage, because they stack the trash bags up into little mountains on the sidewalks in New York."

God, what a bullshitter.

"Catherine loved the city. She couldn't wait to live there."

"I know. She did. And I loved that about her. But, anyway, I just saw her one afternoon on a street corner in SoHo, and introduced myself. I'd never done that before, but there was something about her. Something familiar. That's what I wanted to tell you. I know this is weird, Mrs. Courington, but it was like I knew your daughter the minute I saw her. It was déjà vu, fate, astral influence. Like two trains on concurrent tracks passing each other in the night and two passengers on separate locomotives peering out the windows and spotting each other."

As I said these words, I knew that in truth, two locomotives had, indeed passed, but only one passenger was looking. The other was boxed inside a funeral train.

"You are a writer," she said, with a slight smile. "What did Catherine say to all of this talk of fate?"

"I didn't want to freak her out, so I didn't tell her. God, how I wish I could tell her. I hope this doesn't scare you, but every atom in my being believes we were soulmates."

Mrs. Courington shook her head. "You should have told her. She believed in that, you know, fate and destiny. She loved stories about alternate realities where things worked out differently. It's funny. Catherine always said that she had the sense she'd find her true love right here in Sterling Springs, even though she lived in a city of millions."

I thought about that, rolling it in my head over and over.

"I don't mean to pry, but can I ask what happened? I was just so shocked when I heard the news."

She looked at me and put her hand over her mouth for a moment.

"You don't know?"

"No, I don't."

She looked really old. Her eyes were lined with deep creases. "I'm sorry, I can't talk about it right now. It's just too much. I'm afraid you have to leave now."

"Sure," I said, standing.

"Thanks for the flowers. That was very thoughtful. I'm sorry. I'm so sorry."

I stepped out into the hot afternoon sunlight, and the door closed behind me. The guy across the street turned and looked at me again. I felt so frustrated.

Crossing the street, I approached him.

"Hi," I said. He wore a muscle T-shirt with the word "Raunch" on it. His goatee was uneven; he had shaved too close on the right side and it had left a big gouge where the hair used to be. The unevenness was distracting.

"Yeah?"

"I was just wondering," I said, "How well do you know Mrs. Courington across the street?"

"Well enough," he said, wiping his greasy hands on his jeans.

"Do you know what happened to her daughter?"

"She's dead."

"I know. But *how* did she die."

The guy's eyes grew skinny.

"What business is it of yours, peckerwood?"

"I'm sorry?"

"Why don't you go askin' her mother? What you askin' me for?"

"Never mind," I said, turning back to the van. I climbed in, started the engine and turned it around. The whole time, the guy continued to glare. He was saying something, too, pointing at me, but I couldn't hear him because the windows were up.

After work, I went home and straight downstairs. I pulled the phone bill out of my back pocket and unfolded it. I felt guilty for stealing the thing. I stared at the New York City address. I imagined some old greystone building along a tree-lined street. The building had a lobby with brass mailboxes set into the wall. The phone bill would have been delivered there, waiting for Catherine.

I tore open the envelope. The phone bill was several pages. It had an itemized list of the calls made in the last weeks of May. Many to Illinois, probably to her mother. Dozens to New York numbers, a few to Boston, one to Los Angeles. I thought I should go to New York City, go to the apartment building, and meet her neighbors. Find out how Catherine died.

But then I realized, it didn't matter at all. It didn't matter how she died. I thought of her halo of peace. I thought of the dreams and how she never spoke.

I looked at the phone bill. *Jesus.* The phone bill. At the top of the first page was her number. I picked up my phone and dialed. The first ring. The second. And a third and a fourth and then the voicemail picked up.

"Hi," she said, her voice strong and clear. "This is Catherine. I'm not here right now, but you know what to do."

And then there was the beep and I hung up the line.

Song of the Cicada

"So, what are we going to do, boss?" asked Milford, sipping from a frosty bottle of Coca-Cola. "Show starts in three hours."

"Yeah," added Wintergreen Williams, pencil skinny with a matching mustache. "This ain't good."

"I think we might have to cancel," said Acorn Johnson. He dabbed the sweat on his forehead with a handkerchief.

The mid-August sun was burning over western Iowa, an unrelenting fireball. If you looked at it, you would swear you could see the solar flares leaping up, arcing, and diving back into the inferno. It was not Sahara hot; not Death Valley hot; it was Iowa-in-August hot. And there was a difference. There was a stillness to that heat. The only sounds came from the mechanical swelling of the late summer cicadas in the still trees at the west end of the large gravel parking lot, and, every so often, a car or a truck, passing on the adjacent Lincoln Highway.

The entire orchestra, all thirteen members, stood there on the edge of town, along the side of the highway, gathered around their tour bus, in the dusty parking lot of the Starline Ballroom. Beyond the parking lot, the farmland spread out to the edge of the horizon, an ocean of sun-weary green. The band members paced, looking to Artimus Fowler, their stalwart leader, world-renowned trumpeter, the "troubadour of Harlem," genius composer behind dozens of influential jazz and big band compositions, including the 1932 hit, "55th Street Swing."

Fowler sat on the steps of the tour bus, with the glass gatefold door open. He dragged on a Lucky Strike.

"Boys," said Fowler, his voice like the gravel beneath his two-tone wingtip shoes. "We must remain positive. Jimmy drove to Des Moines. It's only two hours away. He's probably already there. He's probably bought me a new trumpet. It was time, boys. I've been playing Old Faithful since I was twenty-four. I should have retired her years ago."

None of the band said a word. They just looked at their leader while the cicadas in the trees at the end of the parking lot buzzed.

"Jimmy will be back before the gig with a new horn and the show will go on, just like it always does. In fact, it might just be the best show we've ever played. Keep your hopes up, boys—keep your hopes alive."

But even as Artimus Fowler tried to lift the spirits of his band members, he had his own doubts. The night before, in Omaha, his trumpet just vanished, backstage, after the gig. Someone had stolen her.

Every single album he had ever recorded, he had used that trumpet. Just two years earlier, in 1951, he had even recorded an album named for her, "Old Faithful." There she was, gleaming on the cover of the LP, gold and shiny with a stark white backdrop. She looked like the horn that trumpeted the arrival of the faithful at the Pearly Gates.

Artimus Fowler sat on the steps of the bus and a range of memories moved through his head like waves falling on a shoreline.

There was the day his father gave him the trumpet. His twenty-fourth birthday. Artimus was just starting out, all the days of his career before him, like a highway rife with discovery. Everything at that point was an unknown. Would he even make a name for himself in the music business? Standing in the living room of their Harlem apartment, rain beating down on the iron fire escape, Artimus opened the case and saw the instrument in the black velvet-lined box—Pharaoh's treasure exposed to the light. From the mouthpiece to the valves to the perfectly curved bell, she was silent in that case, but she wouldn't remain silent for long. Soon she would sing on a journey that would take her across the world, from the clubs of New York to the USO stages of war-torn Europe.

Young Artimus looked up from the new horn to his father seated on the sofa and saw tears in his father's eyes. Artimus never once saw his father cry before that day, nor after. The son of an enslaved man, his father never had money, but he had worked hard and saved and bought that very expensive trumpet because he believed in his son and his future.

There was the parade of small concerts and performances; his first paid gig; his first session work. Then there was the procession of shows at the Cotton Club—each gig more triumphant than the last. There was the palpable sense of momentum to his career, a passenger train gaining speed, an unstoppable forward trajectory.

Things were looking up. He recorded his first album at Clarion Studio off of Times Square. He soloed alongside Satchmo in Hollywood. He scored several films and soon became a household name.

There were so many memories attached to that trumpet.

And now ... this.

Artimus sighed sitting there on the bus steps.

He had always been a man of conviction and positive thinking. If ever a glass was half-full, it belonged on his table. But his faith and general sunny disposition had been shaded in recent years. After the war had ended, big band music had slowly fallen out of favor, making way for a new generation of popular crooners. Fowler's shows weren't always sold out like they used to be. The albums weren't selling as well. His songs weren't played on the radio stations like they were in the good old days. Critics said that Artimus had lost his edge, his improvisational spirit, his relevance.

Undaunted, the Artimus Fowler Orchestra played on. They toured endlessly and recorded and kept on going as the world changed around them.

Artimus looked at his band, standing around the bus, pacing, hands in their pockets. The insects went on buzzing in the trees. He loosened his necktie.

Tonight, Artimus Fowler knew, was a big night. The show from the Starline Ballroom was going to be a remote broadcast, live, coast-to-coast. This was the chance he and the boys had been waiting for. This was their opportunity to show the world that they still mattered—that big band music still had currency.

But then the trumpet went missing. And would a Des Moines music store be open this late on a Saturday afternoon that would have a suitable replacement? Not just any trumpet would do. He sat there on the steps of the bus and looked at the members of his band, standing out in that damn dusty parking lot, gathered and pacing around that chrome and steel bus.

A man approached from the ballroom. He had his coat off, his sleeves rolled up, his tie loosened.

"Good day, Mr. Fowler," the man said, with a nod, extending his hand. "I'm Jack Worley from KKWZ. We're running the remote tonight and setting up our equipment. Is there anything we need to know about your set or the arrangements?"

Fowler laughed. "No, I suspect the show will be just perfect tonight. We are like a precision Swiss Watch, the boys and I. We play the same sterling set night in and night out."

Fowler stood up from the bus steps and extinguished his cigarette under his shoe. It was then that he noticed a boy, with a short mess of walnut hair, standing some feet away. The boy had his hands in his overall pockets and looked on at the scene, rocking on the balls of his feet, like he was waiting for something. Fowler smiled at him.

"Mr. Fowler, sir, is there any word on finding a replacement for the missing instrument?" asked the man from the radio station.

"No word. But I'm none-too-worried. Our road manager is a bit of a magician in times like these—a regular Harry Houdini."

"That's good. The doors to the ballroom open in two hours."

The radio man returned to the ballroom, walking back across the parking lot. Artimus Fowler looked at the boy, still standing there, still staring at them.

"Come here, son."

The band members all looked on. A freight train whistle blew in the distance.

"What's your name?"

"Wilson Bennett the Third, sir. My friends just call me Three."

"May I call you Three?"

"It would be an honor, sir."

"Are you a fan of my music, Three?"

"I was raised on it, sir. My father was your biggest follower ever. He shared your music with me."

The boy looked at the orchestra members. His eyes were round and unblinking and his mouth slightly agape, as if he were standing before the Gods of Olympus.

"I know every one of your band members, sir. I even have some of their solo records. I know that Wintergreen Williams has been with you the longest and your guitarist John Edgefield, Jr. is your newest member. He joined ten months ago."

John Edgefield, Jr., leaning against the bus with a toothpick in his mouth, his eyes shaded by sunglasses, cocked his head their way.

Artimus Fowler clapped his hands and laughed. "That's mighty impressive. How do you know so much?"

"My father taught me to love everything about you, sir."

"Where's your father? He coming to the show tonight?" asked Fowler. "I should buy that man a right good supper!"

"My daddy died in the war. November 18, 1944. The Battle of Hürtgen Forest. Captain Wilson Bennett, Jr."

"I'm sorry to hear that, son. Very sorry. How old are you, by the way?"

"Ten, sir."

"Why, you couldn't have been out of the crib when your father gave his life for our country. How'd you learn so much about me and the boys, then? I thought you said your father taught you?"

"My father left behind all of your records. I've been listening my entire life."

The band members gathered around the boy and Artimus Fowler. The cicadas continued to buzz, a tree chorus of rising and receding, rising and receding, the same rhythm building and then fading. Fowler stood. He closed his eyes and inhaled deeply. No one said a word.

"One could make a song out of that sound," he said, finally. "That's the rhythm of summer, I reckon."

The entire band, and the boy, stood and listened to the sound of the insects in the still green trees. They stood there in that heat, on that parking lot, and listened to that sound.

"When I was just starting out," said Fowler, "I used to listen to the birds in the park; the rain outside our apartment in Harlem, the sound of the subway coming up from street grates—just about anything. You know, when you put your ear to it, there's music in everything. The world is one big, beautiful orchestra."

Everyone listened to the cicadas.

"Beautiful," said Fowler.

"Mr. Fowler, sir," said the boy. "What was that man from the radio station asking about?"

Artimus Fowler patted him on the shoulder and smiled.

"Three, don't you go worrying. The boys and I will go on just as we always do. We're just missing one of our instruments."

"That's an understatement, boss," said Jet Jackson, the piano player.

Fowler chuckled. "As I was saying, Three, our manager went to Des Moines to pick up the missing equipment and the show will go on just fine."

"I'll be listening on the radio at eight o' clock sharp."

"Tell you what," said Artimus Fowler, his hand still on the boy's shoulder. "Kids ain't allowed into the shows at this ballroom, but that doesn't mean I can't bring you in now and show you the stage and our gear. You want to come see?"

"Do I ever!"

And as the cicadas sang and the late afternoon sun burned, Artimus Fowler walked Wilson Bennett the Third across the dusty parking lot towards the entranceway to the Starline Ballroom.

Inside, it was dim and cool. Workers moved about with precision, preparing the venue for the performance that would begin in a few hours. There were voices of men talking, the sounds of tinkling glassware being polished and placed behind the bar. Small round tables surrounded the large, square parquet floor in the middle of the room. The ceiling was painted like the Midwest night sky, big and expansive, black and indigo with darks puffs of clouds. Small white lights set into the ceiling twinkled like stars.

Artimus Fowler walked his friend towards the stage. Three couldn't believe any of it. All the gear was there, the drums, the piano, the upright bass, and the white and chrome music stands with the bold black initials "AF" printed on them, front and center. They were the same art deco stands that the Fowler Orchestra had used in the early '30s. Three had seen them in photographs on the back of a record album. He walked up closer to the stage and looked at the stands the orchestra members sat behind. Upon closer examination, they showed wear from the years on the road, they were a bit chipped and dented in places—but still—how Three wished his father could have seen all of this.

"Come on stage," Fowler said, ushering Three up a few steps. The boy saw Fowler's microphone, polished and standing center stage. He looked out at the ballroom before him, empty, save the flurry of workers moving about in the hushed darkness.

"I never thought I'd see this view. To stand where you stand."

"Only thing missing," Fowler said, "are about one-thousand people. Let's hope they show up tonight."

"Oh, they will, Mr. Fowler, they will. You are the greatest band leader ever."

"That's kind of you to say, young man, but I'm afraid my kind of music isn't as popular as it once was."

"I think your best album is yet to come."

Fowler loved this kid. He wanted to take him on the road with him. All the despair and the uncertainty were gone with this boy around.

After a time, they went back out to the heat, the late day sun had lowered a fraction. The cicadas still buzzed. Several of the boys in the orchestra had baseball mitts and were playing catch in the parking lot. The ball arched lazily in the air and snapped when it was caught in the leather mitts.

They waited for their road manager to return. An hour passed. Fowler was growing more restless. And while he did his best to mask his mounting anxiety, the members of his orchestra could sense the tension. Then, finally, an automobile rolled in, kicking up clouds of dust. Jimmy, the road manager, had driven to Des Moines with an employee of the ballroom. He stepped out, and they all knew right away that the news was not good. Jimmy shook his head. Fowler's heart sank. The band members stopped playing catch. They all gathered around.

"Ain't no stores open. Not one. We drove all across town. Even hit a couple pawn shops."

Artimus Fowler said nothing. Three, still standing by his side, looked up at him.

"What is it, sir?"

"My trumpet was stolen last night, Three. I guess I don't have a horn to play for the show this evening."

"Old Faithful? You lost Old Faithful?"

"I'm afraid so."

"What are we going to do, Artimus?" asked the road manager.

"The band can play without me, I guess. I'll conduct and introduce the songs. We have to improvise. Might be good for us, show won't be so scripted."

"The show starts in just over an hour. It's being broadcast all over the country. People want to hear Artimus Fowler on trumpet," said Jimmy.

Three tugged on Fowler's shirtsleeve. "Sir?"

"Yes, Three?"

"My father had a trumpet. He never played it. My mother bought it for him as a present for when he returned from the war."

Jimmy patted Three on the back. "That's generous, kid. But Mr. Fowler here played a very expensive, professional grade instrument. He could play your father's horn, but it wouldn't be quite the same."

"But it is the same."

Jimmy looked at the kid. "What are you saying?"

"It's exactly the same horn. My father dreamed of becoming a trumpet player. As a gift for when he came back from Europe, my mama bought him a trumpet. A 1924 Hartman trumpet. The exact make and model played by his hero. You, Mr. Fowler."

Everybody in the parking lot stopped and looked at the boy. It seemed like, for a moment, even the cicadas went quiet.

"Kid," said Jimmy, the road manager. "Let's take a drive over to your house."

~~~

Word had spread throughout the region that the Artimus Fowler Orchestra was playing the Starline Ballroom. And while the popularity of big band music may have been on the wane in the late summer of 1953, the crowd still rolled in. Just past seven, a line of automobiles pulled into the parking lot off the Lincoln Highway. It helped, too, that the town newspaper had written up the show and mentioned that it was the first time that a live national radio broadcast would originate from the Starline Ballroom in Carroll, Iowa.

Another car wheeled into the parking lot, a '49 Kaiser Deluxe, and Jimmy the road manager stepped out, along with the boy holding a black, hard-shell case. The cicadas in the trees continued to buzz, swelling and receding. The sunset creased the horizon.

Backstage in the ballroom, Jimmy rushed in, hustling the boy in front of him.

"Show him, kid, show him."

Wilson Bennett the Third held out the hard-shell case, offering it to Artimus Fowler. The bandleader was dressed in a white coat and a black bow tie.

"Your father's trumpet?"

Three nodded.

Fowler took the case from the boy. He placed the case on his lap and unlatched it. Slowly, he lifted the lid. The lights in the room reflected off the trumpet in one hundred different ways. It was sculpted in brass, perfect brass, gleaming like Solomon's gold. There wasn't a single scratch on her. Looking at that trumpet, Artimus Fowler felt like he was twenty-four again. He could imagine music emanating from that horn. He looked up at Three. The boy was smiling.

"Son, I'm going to make your father proud."

~~~

When the red velvet curtain went up at the Starline Ballroom, Artimus Fowler looked out and was stunned. It was a full house—nearly two thousand people. The biggest crowd the place had seen in a long, long time. The orchestra kicked in with precision. They went in to their first number, "Moon Shadows," and scores of people took to the dance floor, legs and arms and bodies moving in unison to the beat of Wintergreen Williams' drums. Artimus Fowler put his lips to the trumpet and blew, and that first note—the sound, the glory—surprised him. It was strong and youthful. It was like Old Faithful on her first day, that day in Harlem, she was reborn. And Artimus Fowler played that song like a man renewed. Even some of the dancers stopped their movements to watch. The bandleader, now forty-seven, was playing with fire, passion, vigor—a flourish here, an unexpected triplet there. And as they went in to the next number, Artimus Fowler did something unexpected. This man, known for his precision and exactness, started, unexplained to all, even himself, to improvise. Like in the old days. He heard those summer cicadas in his mind, waxing, waning, swelling, receding, ebbing, flowing over and over and over and he started to interpret that sound through that horn.

New Faithful, he thought, as he blew. *New Faithful.*

The thirteen-member orchestra was caught off guard. Live over national radio, Artimus Fowler had taken a melodic detour unlike any they had ever heard. This man was the "Swiss Watch" of Jazz. Reliable. What was he doing? The orchestra had no choice but to try and follow along.

Wintergreen Williams was the first to pick it up. Fowler was playing that summer sound—the song of the cicadas. He heard the rhythm. And he began to beat his snare. And Acorn Johnson played in harmony to the notes that his bandleader blew from that trumpet. And the whole band played along. And the incredulous crowd started to dance to the completely improvised music. And Artimus Fowler let it unfurl and surprise him and go.

And over the microphones and across the airwaves, a new song was carried out of the Starline Ballroom.

In a farmhouse fifty miles away, in Atlantic, an 80-year-old man sat on his front porch in the hot purple twilight and listened to the radio from his living room.

In Chicago, in a third-floor apartment in South Shore, a family of five gathered around the radio and nodded their heads. Artimus Fowler was back.

And in a house high up on Mulholland Drive in Los Angeles, and in a living room in Portland, and in a factory in Toledo, people stopped what they were doing and listened.

And in Harlem, where the great Artimus Fowler had first started out, men and women and children gathered around radios and knew that something important was happening on this night in a ballroom in the middle of Iowa farm country.

And in that small Iowa town, Wilson Bennett the Third, and his mother, sat in the living room of their small house in front of their Philco radio. His mother hugged him. And for the first time, Three heard the glorious sound of his father's trumpet.

Böse

Is it okay if I record this?

Of course.

Thank you. For documentation, can you please state your name, title, and years of employment at the hospital?

My name is Mikayla Walker. I'm a Nurse Practitioner in the Oncology Unit at St. Mary's Hospital in Rockford, Illinois. I've worked at the hospital for eleven years.

Thank you, Nurse. Now, could you please describe for me, in as much detail as possible, the unusual experiences you witnessed a year ago?

Yes, doctor. On January 14, I was making my night rounds. The patient chart indicates it was 11:32 pm. I went into room 1412 to check on an eighty-one-year-old patient, Mr. Ethan Rothenberg. I remember that night clearly—the area was under a winter storm warning. I recall looking out the windows down on the parking lot. It was really coming down. The cars were all buried in snow. I could hardly see them under the lights. I checked on Mr. Rothenberg. He was a stage-four cancer patient. His white blood count had dropped, and he had been

121

administered a transfusion earlier in the day. I checked the lines, to make sure everything was functioning properly with the infusion pump.

Who was working on the floor that night?

There were five of us: Judy Black, Chris Jordan, Nancy Suarez, Alex Ling, and me.

I know you have told me what occurred, but for the sake of this recording, would you describe, again, what happened when you went in to check on the patient?

Yes. I went into room 1412. The lights were off. The infusion pump was beeping, indicating it was functioning properly. I closed the curtains on the windows, since the glow from the streetlights and snow was bright. Mr. Rothenberg had kicked his blanket off, so I tidied up. I took his wrist and listened to his pulse. It was slower than normal. I inspected the IV. The bag was three-quarters empty.

Can you tell me the blood type that was being administered to the patient?

AB negative.

The most rare blood type, found in just one percent of Caucasians and even less in minorities.

Yes.

And what happened next?

Well, after inspecting the line, and confirming the transfusion was administering properly, I turned from the patient, picked up my tablet to enter the information in the system, and walked towards the door.

And then?

It was then that I heard an odd noise.

What did you hear?

A gentle, deep bubbling coming from near the patient. Sort of a softer version of the way an air bubble spontaneously rises in a water cooler.

What did you do?

Well, I thought it was odd. I turned and went back towards the patient in bed. That's when I noticed something.

What did you see?

Something in the blood bag. A large air bubble, churning and moving. The patient remained asleep. I was startled, so I moved closer to the IV. I switched on the lights over the bed and looked at the bag more closely. The air bubble moved again. It was about the size of an orange. It shifted and morphed, round, oval, cylindrical, separating into multiple bubbles and then back into one.

What did you do?

I checked the patient. His vitals were stable. His pulse still in the lower range.

I radioed the nurse's station. At that same time, a code blue was issued on the floor. All staff was needed in room 1451. I would say I don't normally buckle under stress, but, I admit I was worried. I knew that the blood bubbles were dangerous and abnormal, whatever they were, but I also knew that I was needed in room 1451 immediately.

What did you do?

I radioed the nurse's station to inform them that there was an issue with the patient, but they were already on their way to the code blue. As I was opening the door, I saw the nurses and doctors rushing down the hall to the code blue. So I went back into the room. I knew I had to stop the transfusion. Change the blood bag. When I stepped back in, I saw it.

Saw *it?*

Yes.

What?

A face in the bubble of blood. An old face with eyes. It was shifting, blinking, looking directly at me. I was so startled. I went immediately to the IV pump. The face seemed to panic, and it moved quickly in the IV bag, deep into the blood, retreating, shrinking ... then vanished.

What did you do?

I immediately disconnected the IV from the patient.

What were you thinking at that point? You had just seen something unusual, to say the least. A face, you said, looking at you from the transfusion bag—

At first, I thought that it was dark and I was tired, and maybe seeing things. But in the back of my mind, I knew that was highly unlikely.

Were you frightened?

No. I went to retrieve a new transfusion. I switched out the old bag and everything was fine for the rest of the night in room 1412. Of course, it was busy on the unit. We lost the code blue patient. And there was the blizzard.

Did you tell the other nurses what you had seen?

No. The patient's vitals remained stable, so I chalked it up to my mind playing tricks. I'm not as young as I used to be, doctor. Maybe the old brain was just tired. Anyway, everything from that point forward was normal for the patient.

Everything?

Yes. Until forty-eight hours later. The patient died very suddenly. The cause of death was a cerebrovascular accident.

A stroke.

Yes.

After he died, you reported the incident with the IV pump. I learned of it

through your report, as the Chief of the Medical Oncology and Hematology Division.

Yes, that's right. I knew I had to report what I'd seen, since he died so suddenly. To be honest, I was concerned the other nurses and doctors would think I was crazy.

Who did you report it to?

Judy Black, the head nurse.

And what was Nurse Black's response to what you had witnessed in room 1412?

She thought it was fatigue. She said it was a hectic night, and it was, and that my mind was playing tricks on me. She recommended we not add the incident to the patient's file, but did say she would, at the very least, inform you.

She did inform me. I reviewed the file. Nurse, there was no indication that Mr. Rothenberg's death was related to what you saw that night. He died of natural causes.

It does seem coincidental, if you ask me.

This is the reason I am recording our conversation. What I am about to tell you, I have not told anyone.

Doctor?

I had a similar experience to the one you had that night. I have never mentioned it. When Mr. Rothenberg died, you did the right thing, regardless of what people

may have thought about you. You reported what you had seen in the blood transfusion bag. That face.

You saw it?

Something like it. It haunts me.

Is that why you're recording this conversation?

I have a suspicion. Whatever that face was, it has existed for a long time. Others may have seen it, too, but I suspect, have never reported it.

When did you first see it, doctor?

A long time ago, when I was a resident at Smyth Cancer Treatment Center in Houston. I was working the overnight shift. I was exhausted after working 16 hours. It was July and Houston was unbearably hot.

Yes, I know what you mean about the heat. My father was from Sugarland. A Houston summer is worse than a Rockford winter.

The air conditioning units were working overtime. We were told to watch our electrical use closely, dim any unnecessary lights for fear of an outage. Unplug the vending machines in the commissary. It was two in the morning when it happened. The hospital went dark. The generators kicked in as well as the back-up batteries on the medical equipment. We were understaffed that night and when the lights went out, and only emergency lights came on, it was eerie. It felt more like a morgue than a hospital.

What did you do?

I made the rounds, checking on patients to make sure IVs were functioning, respirators, all the vital medical equipment. I will never forget—I checked on a favorite patient of mine, Rose Johnson. Mrs. Johnson had stage-four brain cancer, but she never lost her sense of humor. She was a young mother, two kids.

What happened?

I was checking her vitals when I heard a gurgling sound. I was listening to her pulse when I heard it. At first, I wasn't sure where it was coming from. Then it became more pronounced, as if someone was trying to say something to me, words being spoken from a great distance. It was a very guttural sound. Deep. Then, in my peripheral vision, I saw it. Something in the blood bag. Mrs. Johnson had a very low white blood cell count and was receiving blood. I looked at the IV bag, and there it was, a face staring at me—a woman's face, blinking, mouth moving, causing the sounds I had heard.

Similar to what I saw?

Yes.

What did you do next?

I quickly grabbed the transfusion bag. Whatever was inside, that face made of blood and air, it did not like my rapid movement. I believe this—it took my movement as hostile.

What happened?

Unlike your experience with Mr. Rothenberg, where the face you witnessed vanished in the fluids, my fast movement agitated the thing, whatever it was. It looked at me, that face, I'll never forget—it was a malice I have never seen before. Hate. Anger. Torture. Loathing. It rushed to the edge of the bag and slammed into the sides, its face dispersing into bubbles and then reforming to glare at me. It opened its mouth, and I saw a fence of uneven needle teeth. I jumped back from the IV, fearing it might burst the plastic. I panicked and ran from the room. Within an hour, Mrs. Johnson's vitals took a jagged and very unexpected turn and she died. I have never shared this story with anyone.

What was Mrs. Johnson's blood type?

AB negative.

(SILENCE)

I haven't seen that face again. And I hope I never do.

Yes, I understand.

When your story was brought to me, I knew that the memory from my residency was not a hallucination of an overworked, overtired medical student. I knew the face was real. We saw the same thing.

The face was very real.

It was, and it prompted me to do some research over the years. To see if anyone else has ever seen that face in the blood.

What did you find?

I believe most medical professionals, if they had ever encountered this unspeakable thing, whatever it is—they never reported it. They must have feared being dismissed or deemed insane. It could ruin a career. But since your report was brought to my attention, I have been poring over medical journals.

And?

I found two reports in *The New England Journal of Medicine*—two references to a face in blood. The first, from an army surgeon, during a battle in the Iraq War. She saw the face in the transfusion bag—AB negative. She had successfully operated on a soldier who sustained head injuries after an IED detonated. He later died unexpectedly. Afterwards, she wrote a paper on wartime anxiety and dismissed the sighting of the face to the trauma of war.

You said you found two reports of the face in the *Journal?*

Yes. The second is far more ominous.

What did you find?

The research of Dr. Wilhelm Liek, published posthumously in June 1962.

The Nazi cancer scientist?

Yes. The article is lengthy and was very controversial upon its publication. But Liek did a great deal of research into cancer that is, today, being reluctantly recognized as astute, if irresponsible and inhumane. He has been universally condemned for his human experimentation.

But you said he saw a face in blood?

He did. Liek spent many years researching homeopathy and natural foods and their influence on cancer cell growth rates. He dedicated a great deal of time to finding a cure to cancer. Liek experimented with mutating cancer cells in various ways. In his report, he firmly believed that his lab work actually caused cancer cells to become sentient, to become thinking and feeling, in a patient he was studying—blood type AB negative. Liek believed he inadvertently caused the cancer cells he was working with to become alive and, if you will, personified. He saw the face in transfusions on numerous occasions, each time referencing it as "Böse."

Böse?

Evil.

Good Lord.

I believe that Liek, during his research, brought cancer to life. He was working on a patient, blood type AB negative, when this occurred. He saw the face in the blood. And to this day, some of these cancer cells are still, for some reason, with us, in the blood supply. We both saw it.

Doctor, what happened to Liek?

He was injured at the end of World War II, during a bombing. His own team treated him. He had sustained considerable internal injuries, so they gave him a transfusion. He died twenty-four hours later.

He was AB negative?

Yes. He actually sketched two drawings of the face he witnessed and took a photo. The grainy photo is inconclusive and has been largely dismissed over the years, but his sketches are concerning. They bare an unmistakable resemblance to Liek himself. As I think about these different cases—the face I saw, it was a woman. It could well have been Mrs. Johnson's. Nurse, you stated that you saw an old man. Did it resemble Mr. Rothenberger?

It might have. Doctor …

Yes?

I had a second experience with the face in the blood. Last week. I didn't report it yet.

Nurse, you should have told me this immediately.

I know.

What happened?

I was retrieving a blood bag from refrigeration, to take to a patient's room. As I was holding it, the bag lurched. It moved. It startled me. I looked down and saw it. A man's face. Younger than the one I had seen that night with Mr.

Rothenberg. It was glaring at me. But it looked familar. It opened its mouth and then bit the edge of the bag. I screamed and dropped it, and it exploded, blood everywhere, all over my hands, all over me. I reported it as a mistake and faulty transfusion bag, but it wasn't that at all.

Dear Lord.

Doctor?

Yes, Nurse?

Before the bag exploded, I noticed something about the face. I ... please understand, I don't know what to make of this. That face. It was so evil. Like you said. But it looked so familiar. Now that I think about it, to be honest, I knew that face. It reminded me of someone ...

Nurse?

If it's not too personal, may I ask, what blood type are you?

Night Summons

Mrs. Angeline Kinney pulled the lace curtain back and peered out through the library window. Beyond the leaded glass panes, it was misting outside. The burnt-tip orchids in the garden wilted slightly under the weight of the late afternoon precipitation. Little droplets of rain gathered on the petals, mottling them red and white. Beyond the garden was a thicket of yew bushes, and, beyond that, the rolling grasslands of the Salisbury Plain, and somewhere beyond that, monolithic stones standing thousands and thousands of years. It was remote and quiet and peaceful living out here.

Mrs. Angeline Kinney's chest heaved ever so slightly. She touched her fingers to her lips. Letting go of the curtain and moving to the settee, she sat and lit a cigarette. She opened a book, *The English Countryside*. The mantle clock ticked.

Soon, Mr. Kinney arrived home, hanging his hat, removing his gray trench coat. He placed his umbrella in a tall wicker basket in the corner of the entranceway. He was slender, never slouched, and his clothes were hardly wrinkled, even after a long day. He strode down the hallway.

"Hello, dearest. How was your day?" he said, moving past his wife toward the crystal bottles of liquor on a chrome rollaway cart. Taking some ice cubes from a bucket carefully, he clinked them in the highball and poured himself a scotch.

"My day was lovely, really," said Mrs. Angeline Kinney. "What about yours?"

"Glorious," he said, sipping his drink and not once looking at her.

Mrs. Angeline Kinney watched her husband as he sipped his drink. She dragged on her cigarette.

"Are you hungry, dear?"

"Yes, of course," he said, sipped his cocktail, and turned towards her. "Thank you."

Mrs. Angeline Kinney went to the kitchen and pulled the roast from the oven. Roast that he had requested for so many years. Not too much salt. Only a dash of pepper, or else it would upset his stomach. How many nights had she done this? Their life was like a machine of absolute precision.

She reminded herself that, despite these thoughts, she was fortunate. She had this idyllic cottage in the wilds of south central England. And Mr. Kinney was a good and decent man who made a decent wage and who never once questioned her.

He lit the long-tapered candles on the dining table. They ate, in silence, save for the occasional outburst of small-talk chatter and the tinkling of silver on china.

"This was delicious, dear," he said, standing after the meal to clear the table. "Thank you."

They retired to the library to read. The stillness was interrupted, only once, by the buffeting of helicopter blades overhead, a night mission from the nearby Middle Wallop Army Air Corps Base.

"They're flying later than usual tonight," said Mr. Kinney, not looking up from his book.

Mrs. Angeline Kinney considered her husband. He really hadn't aged much over the years. In many ways, he was more handsome than ever—no longer the gangly young man she had married at Bath Abbey so long ago. Instead, he had filled out, grown up, grown into his years.

He looked up and his eyes met hers.

"What is it, dear?"

"You're quite handsome."

He paused for a moment.

"Why, thank you, dear." He said nothing more and returned to reading.

She almost smiled. Did she expect him to return the praise?

They carried on until it was bedtime, and then they drew the curtains and dimmed the lights. Mrs. Angeline Kinney went to the bathroom and sat before the mirror and washed her face clean of the day's make-up. She looked at herself. Looked at the wrinkles on her hands, the sagging around her eyes and neck.

My, how I have aged.

As she looked at herself, it felt like she was still talking to the eight-year-old girl who once sat before her mother's vanity.

"I love you," she said, under her breath.

"What was that, darling?" asked her husband, tying the sash of his robe behind her.

She was slightly startled that her husband had heard her.

"I said that I'm quite tired." Mrs. Angeline Kinney turned to the bedroom, her voice slightly raised.

"Yes, I'm sure you are."

The couple retired to bed. Mr. Kinney turned the switch on the lamp on the end table and they rested in darkness. Within minutes, Mr. Kinney began snoring. Mrs. Angeline Kinney, resting on her back, stared at the ceiling. She turned. She flipped to her side and looked out the window at the poplar trees in the distance, and she thought of the vastness of the chalk grassland and everything beyond. A light mizzle of rain fell and, just as she always did, Mrs. Angeline Kinney fell asleep to the sounds of her husband's slumber.

Morning came and the hot tea and poached eggs and the barely toasted toast.

"Have a good day," Mr. Kinney said, kissing his wife on the top of her head, and then he got in his sedan and drove off as his wife stood in the doorway and watched the car move down the long, curving road, becoming ever smaller until, at last, it disappeared over a rise.

She put the dishes away, dressed, and put on her make-up with care. And then she moved to the window and pulled the curtains to the side. Two plump warblers skittered about the yard. At last, the birds landed in the branches of a gnarled hawthorn tree. The sky was blue, full of lofty, bilious clouds. Beyond the yard, past the grass and flowers and wall of green, was the wind-swept grass landscape of the plain—putty colored, rolling and stretching out to the horizon.

What day is this?

She thought of her life, the sixteen years of marriage and nary a minute of spontaneity or whimsy or downright splendid insanity.

At dinner, she looked across the table to her husband.

"Why don't we go to London this weekend, dear?" she asked.

"Whatever for?" he said, a look of surprise on his smooth, clean-shaven face.

"We could go to Chinatown for dinner! It has been so long since we did that. And afterwards we could walk to the theater district to see a show!"

Mr. Kinney laughed, his shoulders rising up and down as he chortled through his nostrils.

"Perhaps another time," he said. "It has been a long week already, dear."

A serious look crossed Mrs. Angeline Kinney's face. Her lips thinned and she spoke, her voice raised. "You don't take me out anymore. I can't even re-member the last time we were in London."

Mr. Kinney set his fork down. There was a canyon of silence across the dining table. "Dear," he said, at last. "This is the quiet life we always dreamed of. We have our country home and our country existence. Why we never had children. You wanted this as much as I. We were both solitary people before we met and, now, well, we are a solitary couple. I thought you liked it this way?

Don't you, Angeline? Don't you like it this way? Because I do. I like our life. I like it very much."

Mrs. Angeline Kinney stood from the table and lifted her plate.

"No, I don't like it at all."

Startled, Mr. Kinney watched as his wife carried her plate into the kitchen.

That night, in bed, Mrs. Angeline Kinney rested on her side, in a half-curl, with her back to her husband. He was awake, still. She could feel it. Besides, there was the absence of snoring. She closed her eyes tightly and on the inside of her lids she could see little electric cobalt sparks, ocular floaters she could not look directly at or they would retreat.

The next day was the same, and the next, and the next. The breakfast, and the books, and the window, and the arrival of Mr. Kinney, and the dinner, and the candles, and the conversation that made her feel even more remote and, finally—bed. The infernal machine of their marriage.

And then, one night, she awoke before dawn. Mr. Kinney was, of course, snoring. Rain pattered on the stone tile roof. A tumbling of distant thunder. She sat and put her feet down on the soft rug. She looked back at her husband. He was deeply slumbering, blanketed in the cobalt light of the pre-dawn hours.

Mrs. Angeline Kinney felt it, the pull of the English countryside. She felt it as she walked out of the bedroom and to the front door. She felt it as she lifted her raincoat off the rack. She felt it as she slipped on her shoes and opened the door. She saw that the rain was coming down harder, and the sky flashed with distant lightning, but she stepped out anyway.

Mrs. Angeline Kinney walked out into her yard, passing the flowers. She reached the thicket of shrubbery at the periphery, found an opening, and pushed the damp limbs aside and ventured through. Branches clawed at her wrists and her ankles, drawing crisscrossing lines of blood. She felt the pain and she thought, "Thank goodness. I felt that."

She emerged through the wall of bushes and ventured onto the field beyond. The wind kicked up, stirring the bottom of her coat and her hair. Thunder rolled as the sky roiled a dozen shades of dark. There was an ironclad determination about her, but she did not think about that. She knew that she had to walk. She could not explain it. She did not question it.

She just kept walking. The tall grass dampened her shoes and her legs. Within minutes, her hair was soaked from the rain. How long she walked, she did not notice. Where she was going, she was not sure. It was just that, well, she felt pulled.

She traversed the gently rolling landscape. She was soaked through, like a sponge needing to be wrung. The thunder overhead grew more ominous. The dark clouds moved and reformed and rolled. A branch of lightning cracked and the sky lit. Mrs. Angeline Kinney moved with urgency now, faster, faster. She staggered down a grassy slope towards a small two-lane road. The rain was falling harder now. She crossed the road and moved up a gentle incline. She was closer now. Closer. She could feel it. Thunder walloped above. Mrs. Angeline Kinney's foot lunged down into a pockmark and she fell.

Sprawled in the mud and the grass, she lifted her head as the night illuminated for a brief moment and she saw it. The vastness of the plain. And it. Alone. Looming. Off in the distance.

And then it went dark again. And then more lightning. And she knew, now, where she was.

Stonehenge.

The monolith stood in the night, as it had for more than 2,500 years. Mrs. Angeline Kinney did not move. She could not look away.

Behind her, down the distant road, came two pin pricks of light. An automobile. Mrs. Angeline Kinney did not notice. She stared at the monument. She wept in the rain. And she laughed. It just seemed as if—it seemed so silly—that she had been summoned. Why? She had no clue.

The headlights grew bigger. The car drew closer, going up the gentle slope of the road and then down, disappearing momentarily, only to reemerge, closer, ever closer.

The car arrived and skidded to a halt on the pea-gravel shoulder. Wiper blades thumped in unison across the windshield. Drops of rain showered down in front of the wide beams of the head lamps. The driver's side door opened and Mr. Kinney stepped out, lowering the fedora, shielding his face from the downpour.

"Angeline!" he cried to the darkness. "Angeline! Where are you?"

She heard a voice. A distant voice. Another crack of lightning.

"Angeline!"

Still lying in the grass, she wheeled on her haunches.

Mr. Kinney ran through the field and up the hill towards her. In the flashes of lightning, he saw his wife, and there, beyond, were the looming structures of Stonehenge. The towering slabs of stone were slick with rain and surrounded, at the base, by coils of mist. He sprinted to her.

"Angeline! What on earth are you doing out here? Are you alright? Whatever has gotten into you?"

He reached his hand down to his wife, to help her up. She was drenched, and he was soaked, as well.

"But however did you know?" she asked. "How did you know I was here?"

Mr. Kinney was flummoxed. Incredulous. "Why I ... I don't know. I just did." He extended his hand closer. "Come home, my dear. I love you."

She stood and he hugged her tight.

"And I love you, Timothy. I do. I do."

And Mr. Timothy Kinney helped Mrs. Angeline Kinney up, off the soaked chalkland of the Salisbury Plain. He put his arm around her and they walked back towards the car, the wiper blades still moving rhythmically, the headlights beaming out into the rainy night.

~~~

Days later, London was more alive than she could ever recall. The streets were crowded with people and an unpredictable energy. There was laughter and conversation and activity, everywhere. Angeline Kinney and her husband walked arm in arm in the night, rounding the corner at Gerrard Street and entering London's Chinatown, all the neon storefront lights shining bright.

Roadside Cross

He had passed by it many times over the years, to and from work at the factory, yet he had never noticed it.

It was after midnight, and Tom was returning home on the twenty-mile stretch from the factory to his apartment, driving down County Highway X. The headlights reflected on it, for just a moment—a small white cross, nearly obscured in the thistle along the roadside.

That's strange, Tom thought. *Why have I never seen that before?*

Perhaps the overgrown brush had previously hidden the small wooden marker. It was only about two feet tall, easily veiled in the bramble. The cold wind could have made a clearing, Tom figured, or a deer might have trampled the brush, exposing it. Whatever the reason, Tom didn't think about it further as the pick-up truck passed by.

He tapped his fingers on the steering wheel as an old Ralph Stanley bluegrass song played over the radio band, an AM station, the only station in town with a decent signal. The song was "Hemlocks and Primroses," about a girl who had gone away. A girl with dark hair and lively eyes.

~~~

The next night, after punching out on the time clock at the sheet metal factory, the same time as he always did, Tom headed home. He drove down

County Highway X and listened to old country music on the radio. This time, he hummed along to a slow Hank Williams number. And he saw it, again. The cross.

Of course, Tom had seen these side-of-the-road markers before. He knew their meaning. They were pillars to the deceased. He knew that some loved one, some family member, a friend had placed that cross there, beside that two-lane Wisconsin road. This was where someone had died.

Had it been a drunk-driving accident? Had someone fallen asleep behind the wheel? Maybe the accident had occurred on a winter day when the road was layered with an imperceptible sheen of black ice. Tom wondered who had died along that lonesome stretch of highway.

Passing the cross, he thought of Anabelle Limón. She was just out of community college when she came to work at the factory. She worked in the office, with Tom, filing purchase orders and taking care of other paperwork. They laughed together a lot, over stories of them as kids trying to escape the boredom of their quiet lives. She once climbed a corn silo with friends and had lost a shoe and had to walk home, hopping along the rocky and bristly roads for what she said seemed miles. He told her how he'd joined a rowdy crowd of boys one night and they tipped over a large, decrepit headstone with no name.

She made Tom feel young again, like a boy with a schoolyard crush. He never said anything to her about his feelings, since she was always talking about a boy she liked. Occasionally they had coffee together, or went outside on cold, starry nights for a breath of air.

Anabelle died just a year after she was hired. Some claimed it was drugs, but Tom refused to believe that. She was fresh-faced, often wearing her long black hair loose and shaking it when she laughed. Her eyes lit like the fire inside her. For some reason, driving by that cross made Tom think of her.

A month went by. Some nights, he looked at the cross, illuminated momentarily in the conical white glow of the truck's headlamps. There were nights, lost in the tinny music over the radio, or lost in his thoughts, he forgot to look at it altogether.

On a wind-swept November night, Tom was headed home. The moon hung low, big and orange. Fallen leaves, brittle as ancient papyrus, flittered across the highway. All the surrounding farm fields, shorn down to the earth for the coming winter, were in shadows. There was not much out here, on this drive between the factory and Tom's rented apartment above the hardware store on Main Street. Flashing by the windows on the drive were a few barns, stark yard lights aglow, some grain silos, an abandoned one-room schoolhouse from long ago, and the infrequent farmhouse cast in darkness, the inhabitants asleep. There was a small cemetery, too—Hinkston's Crossing—at the intersection of County Highway X and Hinkston Road. A stitching of black wrought iron fence, with sharp points at the top of each post, surrounded the perfectly square graveyard. Cement and marble headstones, some new, most timeworn, dotted the tiny, well-manicured parcel of earth.

On that November night, when Tom drove past the small wooden cross and the headlights cast light onto it, he saw it—flowers at the base of the cross. Wrapped in butcher paper, the flowers were propped up against the cross. Someone had been there recently.

In the days that followed, as Tom drove past, he looked. The cut flowers browned and wilted. And it rained, and they became damp and sad. Tom wondered who had come out there, who had ventured out to that spot and placed those flowers by that small roadside cross?

~~~

A year went by. Tom had gotten a raise at work. Business was good at the factory. Production was up. He bought a new pickup. He still listened to vintage country music and he still took Highway X home. A light November rain came down; the windshield wipers thumped out of sync with Patsy Cline's crooning. The weather had begun to turn and the trees had lost most of their leaves and the moon was waxing.

The white cross flashed briefly in the headlamps. Tom saw another bouquet propped against it. And something else, something that glimmered briefly as he drove past.

Tom slowed the truck, pulled over to the shoulder, and stepped out. Pea gravel crunched under his work boots. The autumn moon was partially obstructed by a slow-moving cloud.

Tom walked down the drainage culvert and up the other side, into the sun-faded grasses and spiky thistle. He approached the cross, wooden and weathered. The white paint had blistered and was peeling. The flowers were fresh. White lilies and purple hyacinths. Next to them were a dusty wine bottle and a crisp white envelope.

Kneeling down on a knee, he turned the bottle so he could read the label. It was French. Bordeaux. 1928.

A jackrabbit bounded from the brush nearby, scurrying off into the night. It gave Tom's heart a start. Far off, in the distance, a train whistle blew. An Amtrak train, in its nightly route west. Tom looked up and could see the locomotive, silvery in the moonlight, passing, far off on the horizon, tiny squares of light illuminating the windows. *The passengers are all safe and warm*, he thought.

Tom looked back at the wine and the flowers and the cross. He picked up the envelope. It was unsealed. Gently, he removed a small folded slip of paper and opened it. There was but a single handwritten line, in a spidery scrawl: *My sorrow is as lasting as my love.*

He slipped the paper back into the envelope.

He stood and looked at the memorial for a moment, and then walked back to his truck.

~~~

Throughout the next year, on his way to the factory in the late afternoon, driving along County Highway X, Tom would turn and look over his shoulder out of the driver's side window. It was there, as it always was, the cross. There was no bouquet of fresh cut flowers leaning against it. No bottle of wine. Tom wondered if the person would bring them that night? Or the next? Who was this person who came out to the remote farmland each autumn to place a handful of flowers at the base of an unmarked roadside cross? Who brought an ancient bottle of Bordeaux and left it in the field next to the flowers? And that note?

Just after Halloween, with the moon out, Tom drove his truck down Highway X. It was getting cold, leaves were flying across the highway. The truck passed the old abandoned one-room schoolhouse. Passed Hinkston's Crossing and the cemetery with the gravestones in silhouette. Tom neared the location of the roadside cross. He lifted his boot-clad foot off the accelerator. The headlights played across the shoulder of the road.

And they were there, leaning against the cross: a bouquet and a bottle.

Tom pulled over and put the truck in park. Johnny Cash sang about freight trains and prisons.

He ventured out to the cross. The flowers were the same, lilies and hyacinths wrapped in butcher paper. They were so fresh that droplets of water had beaded on the petals. Smelling them, Tom thought they smelled so alive. And at the base of the cross was another bottle of Bordeaux, 1928.

His mind raced. Why that year? Was that the year the deceased had been born? He thought it must have been a grieving lover who left the flowers and wine. An envelope at the base of the cross. A handwritten message scrawled inside. It was the same.

Someone had come to the roadside cross in the time he had gone to work and returned home. It was November 8th. This was the day of mourning.

~~~

The next night at work, Tom sat at his desk, thinking. The sound of the factory beyond the glass windows of the office was muted, a synchronized cacophony. Machinery moved beyond the large window; presses and assembly equipment and vehicles glided back and forth. There was something comforting about all of that automation, something safe. Tom had finished his nightly paperwork when the office door opened. A man in a yellow hard hat entered.

"How are things going, Javier?" Tom asked.

"Hydraulic pressure on press three is acting up again. I shut it down and left a voicemail with the manufacturer."

Tom pushed back from his desk and stood.

"Javier, you live in Sterling Springs. Do you take Highway X home?"

"Sometimes. Other times, I drive down Sterns Road, just to break it up. Why?"

"A couple of years ago I noticed a little roadside cross off the side of the highway. You know, one of those markers someone places in the location where a person died? I'd never seen it there before."

"They're pretty common. Especially out on country roads."

"Yeah," said Tom. "But a few years ago, on November 8th, some flowers appeared by the cross. Then, last year, flowers and a bottle of wine. There was a handwritten note, too. I got out of my truck and looked at it."

"That's sad, man," said Javier. "I'm going to step out for a smoke—you want to come?"

They went out in front of the factory and lit cigarettes. The night was chilly and the stars in the sky were bright. Tom raised the collar of his coat.

"So what I was saying about that cross on the roadside," he said. "A few days ago, on November 8th, another bouquet showed up, along with another old bottle of red, same year, 1928."

Javier exhaled a cloud of smoke. "You ever hear of the Poe Toaster?"

Tom shook his head. "No."

"Well, sometime in the '30s, as the legend goes, a mysterious person began showing up at Edgar Allan Poe's grave. In Baltimore. Every year. January 19th—Poe's birthday. This person, dressed in black, wearing a wide-brimmed hat and white scarf, brought three roses and a bottle of cognac. Poured a glass of brandy and raised it in Poe's honor."

Javier dragged on his cigarette. Finally, he continued. "Years went by, and there were people who wanted to know who this night visitor was. Others wanted to leave him alone. Someone got a picture of him once." Javier turned to Tom. "But they never identified him. The man—they called him 'the Poe Toaster,' stopped showing up a few years back. Some thought he died."

Javier paused. Tom was staring off in the distance.

"Your story reminds me of that," said Javier. "I think a mourner deserves to cry in solitude, Tom. You don't want to know who's leaving the flowers by the roadside cross, do you?"

Tom was silent for a while.

"I do, actually," Tom said. "That cross makes me think of Anabelle Limón. And her death. You know, Javier, I never told anyone this, but I always had a feeling Anabelle and I could have ended up together. Crazy, I know. But I just had that feeling. After she died, we never heard if there was a memorial. Nothing in the paper. The family never contacted anyone here. She was just … gone. It's bothered me."

"Maybe you should find where Anabelle is buried and bring some flowers and wine to her grave, too," said Javier gently.

Tom rubbed a hand through his hair. "I wish I could make the person coming out to that cross, whoever it is, feel better."

Javier crushed his cigarette under his boot.

"Let the grieving grieve."

~~~

But the following year, just after Halloween, as it got colder and the leaves fell and the moon came out, Tom left work one night, several hours early, just before dark. It was November 8th. He drove down Highway X. The sky was turning black, with a crease of orange on the distant horizon. There was the hint of a far-off bonfire in the air.

About a mile away from the cross, just before Hinkston's Crossing cemetery, Tom fiddled with the radio, looking for a good vintage country song. As his index finger pressed the "Seek" button, he took his eyes off the road. And in that brief time, the truck veered to the right, onto the gravel shoulder. Tom heard the stones under the tires; he could feel the rough grade through the heavy-duty tires, through the chassis of the truck, through the soles of his boots, and throughout his body. He jerked the steering wheel hard to the left, to bring the pickup back onto the two-lane highway. And he looked up and he saw her.

A woman in a long, dark dress. She wore a hat—wide brimmed and plumed, pulled low over her face.

She was right in front of the truck.

When she turned to face his truck, Tom jerked the wheel violently, but it was too late. The pickup roared in upon her as she wheeled around. What little Tom could make of her face in the moment was odd. She was expressionless. And her eyes. He swore. She had no eyes. Just gouged-out black holes where they should have been.

The truck hit her head on. Yet there was no crash, no jolt, no body hitting the front grill and falling under the wheels or rolling up and over the hood. Nothing.

Tom slammed on the brakes. The truck skidded to a violent halt.

"Holy Christ!"

Tom leapt from the truck and ran out to look on the roadway. He walked behind his idling vehicle. The red tail lights cast a hellish glow. But there was nothing. No sign of the woman. She had completely and utterly vanished.

Tom's hands were shaking, his heart hurtling within his rib cage. He turned and looked up the highway. Just another hundred yards or so—the roadside cross. He walked toward it, hands still quivering.

He neared it. And they were there. Flowers and wine and envelope. Tom stood knee-deep in the hay-colored brush, not moving.

~~~

Tom went back to the factory. He found Javier on the floor as vehicles moved about and glowing red cinders showered down. Javier wore a hard hat and protective goggles. He turned and saw Tom.

"I thought you went home?" Javier said as he closed the office door.

"Javier, listen to me. The damnedest thing just happened. I can't explain it."

"What?"

"Remember the roadside cross I told you about last year and what you said about the Poe Toaster?"

Javier looked at the office calendar hanging on the wall. November 8th.

"You didn't let the griever grieve."

"I wanted to see who it was. Who puts those flowers out by that cross with that old bottle of wine every year?"

"Did you get your answer?"

"Javier, I was driving down Highway X. I took my eyes off the road for just a second—a split second—and I struck a woman! A woman dressed in black. She turned just as the front of my truck barreled into her."

"*Dios mío.*"

"That's not all. As she turned to look at me, as the truck hit her, she went right through it. Like mist. She just vanished."

Javier was quiet for a moment.

"*Fantasma.*"

"What?

"A ghost."

"I thought about that, too. But that's impossible."

"Is it?"

"This is insane."

"Tom, if the woman truly passed right through your truck and just vanished, there really is no other explanation. *Fantasma.*"

Tom paced the office. Ran his fingers through his crew cut. He poured a cup of warm coffee from the coffeemaker in the corner.

"I walked up to the roadside cross after that. It was just a hundred yards away. The flowers were there. And the wine. And the note. If this ghost—this *fantasma*—is real, is she the one putting them there?"

Javier didn't respond.

"Javier—do ghosts mourn the dead?"

Javier was leaning against a filing cabinet. "La Llorona."

"What did you say?"

"In Mexican folklore, we call her La Llorona. The Weeping Woman. There are different versions of the legend, but basically she mourns the death of a loved one. Other cultures have a legend like that."

"I guess the Midwest has its own version," said Tom. "I hit her with my truck."

"Leave her alone, Tom," said Javier. "She is not a happy spirit. I'll say it again: Let the griever grieve."

~~~

The following year, with the arrival of autumn, Tom kept thinking of the woman. As the days grew short and cold, he couldn't resist. November 8th fell on a Saturday, and he had the day off from the factory. He drove out to the cemetery on County Highway X. There was a small driveway outside the black wrought iron gate. Tom killed the headlights. He waited in the truck until the gray-flannel daylight turned to pitch-darkness. The night was overcast. There were no stars in the sky, no moon. Just as Tom reached for the door handle, to step out of the truck, he saw her, across the field of marble gravestones in the cemetery.

The woman wearing the long black dress and the wide-brimmed hat.

She moved among the graves. She was carrying a bouquet of lilies and hyacinths and a bottle of dark red wine. Her strides were deliberate, like those of a bride marching down the aisle.

"Sweet Jesus," Tom said under his breath, watching her from a distance.

The woman made her way across the small cemetery.

Tom stepped from his truck and walked through the gates, onto the hard grass. Standing next to a scattered row of headstones, he watched her moving among the graves. She didn't notice him. Tom's eyes were fixed on her and he watched, incredulously, as she walked up to the iron fence. Her body moved through the fence without effort, as easily as someone's hand moving through vapor. She walked away from Hinkston's Crossing, onto the shoulder of Highway X.

Tom watched her as she walked off into the night. He was standing on a grave. He looked down at the white marble headstone before him: *Anabelle Limón.*

Oh, God!

Tom couldn't believe it. Any of it.

"Anabelle," he whispered.

His mind raced. The woman in mourning had nothing to do with Anabelle. Tom knew that. But he mourned, just as she mourned.

When Tom looked back up, the woman had gone. He walked around the cemetery and onto the shoulder of County Highway X. The woman was a good distance in front of him, still moving like a bride, slow and methodical.

Let the griever grieve.

But he couldn't. He wished he could take a picture. But he knew the camera on his cell phone wouldn't capture her.

She made her way along the gravel shoulder of the road until the wooden roadside cross came into view. Still clutching the flowers, she moved down the slight bank, across the grassy culvert and across the field. Tom stopped on the shoulder. She moved through the tall brush to the cross and sank to her knees before it. Tom thought he could hear her, thought she was saying some words.

He walked down the embankment, careful to not make noise, and drew closer to the woman. Her voice cracked. He couldn't make out the words. Was it another language? Was she sobbing? Behind him, on the highway, a car sped by, its headlights playing across the field, gliding over Tom and the woman and the cross. Tom froze. The car passed by. The woman did not turn. She continued kneeling before the cross. She leaned the flowers against it. She placed the envelope on the ground.

Tom edged closer. What was she saying? He was now behind her, just some feet away.

The woman stopped speaking. She raised her head. Cold ran through Tom's body. She slowly stood. Turned. Tom looked deep into her gouged-out eyes.

The woman let out a horrible scream—not a scream of fear but a viscous, animal-like night terror, a shrill death siren, like something being tortured. It echoed across the field and the highway and the night.

Let the griever grieve.

He turned in an instant, like a jackrabbit, and ran toward the highway.

She screamed again. Tom turned back. She had raised a finger at him and was taking steps in his direction. He ran toward the highway, years of cigarettes catching up to him.

And there was that horrific scream again. Piercing. Tom ran down the slight embankment, the drainage area alongside the road.

She screamed once more. He turned to look and, impossibly, she was almost upon him.

Tom ran as fast as he could up the embankment to the shoulder of County Highway X. She was just behind him, reaching out with that skeletal hand. Her hand grabbed his shoulder; it was frigid and hard. *Real.*

"Get away from me!" he yelled, and he ran out onto the asphalt highway.

And in that moment, he saw the headlights of the oncoming truck. Bright, otherworldly, ethereal. He heard the great blare of the air horn. The truck hit him straight on.

~~~

Five days later, there was a fresh plot at Hinkston's Crossing. The rectangle of dirt had just been filled in. The freshly dug grave was next to where Anabelle Limón rested. The employees from the factory had come to pay their respects, to say good-bye. They had all thought it was tragic, how two great employees from the factory had died and how they had been laid to rest, next to each other.

After the service, they had left and the cemetery was still. It was dusk and the first light snowfall of the season powdered the new grave. Snow gathered on the headstones, too, and atop the spikes on the posts of the old wrought iron fence.

And a half mile away, along County Highway X, next to a white roadside cross, there was now a matching wooden marker, hammered into the hard earth. Javier dusted the soil from his hands. He picked up the small spade and the mallet, and he walked back to his car along the roadside.

The Key to the City

On a quaint side street in Santa Monica, California, there stood a stucco bungalow that had a yard sale on the first Sunday of every month. The house was compact, with a Spanish-tiled roof and a front yard of loamy Bermuda grass and cascading purple bougainvillea on a front trellis.

The owner of the house, an old woman wearing a silk gypsy scarf of many colors and long, curly false eyelashes, set up tables in the yard before most people were awake. She had just a whisper of a European accent. No one knew where she gathered her wares, a monthly mélange of junk and gems, pop culture curios and antiques from eras far and wide, Victorian, Edwardian, Art Deco, Modern, post-modern, post-post modern, and stuff from Target.

Darlene loved this monthly yard sale. She was sixteen, full of hope and light. She rode a robin's egg blue vintage bicycle with a wicker basket on the handle bars, often in sundresses and sandals.

Darlene knew the old adage that arriving early, before anyone else, was the key to finding the really cool items. Her Great Aunt June, who had introduced her to the joys of these sales and had passed in her sleep last year, used to pat her cheek when she said this.

Darlene dismounted her bike and lowered the kickstand. The old woman who ran the monthly yard bazaar had grown to expect her. She looked forward to seeing the girl with the Fourth of July sparkler personality, first thing in the morning.

"Good morning, dearie," said the old woman, still placing items out on folding tables. An old transistor radio played 1930s swing music.

"Hello, Vadoma! What secret treasures await me today?" Darlene said, her eyes darting over the items. "That lead shot from the Battle of Saratoga—I turned it into a necklace. I looped a leather strand around it. See?"

Darlene reached for a string around her neck. A heavy piece of rounded dark metal hung from it.

"That is wonderful!" said Vadoma. A lap dog trailed her feet, white and puffy, a ball of dryer lint.

"Good morning, Moo Shu!" Darlene reached down to pet the dog's head.

Darlene scanned the items that Vadoma had already placed on the tables. She picked up each item carefully and inspected it. The assortment of milky-green jadeite and multi-colored Fiestaware and some choice Bakelite jewelry fascinated her. She was especially taken by a ring that fit perfectly.

"Where do you find all of these things, Vadoma? It's incredible, really." Darlene often marveled.

"Here and there and around the bend," Vadoma responded, as if in a trance. "In between couch cushions. Buried treasure from long ago. Unearthed cornerstones. Under fallen meteorites. Pawn shops. Curiosity shops. Swap meets. Estate sales. At the bottom of magician's top hats. Beach combing with my metal detector, you know ..."

Darlene smiled and looked over the items on the tables with complete concentration. Glass vases. VHS tapes. Spider Man comic books. Old political buttons. A trumpet. A 1932 Remington typewriter. Cookie jars. Service medals from World War II. Poker chips from the Sands Hotel in Las Vegas. 1970s metal lunchboxes adorned with classic cartoon characters. And, then, situated in the middle of it all, like a masterpiece book buried in the stacks of a labyrinthine library, Darlene spied an oversized ornamental gold key, slightly shorter than her forearm, electro-plated in gleaming gold.

She picked it up. It was heavy in her small hand.

"This is so neat," she said. "What do you suppose this key is for?"

Vadoma shrugged her shoulders. "Maybe it belonged to a giant and it is the key to his castle in the clouds? I might have three beans here somewhere I could sell you."

Vadoma looked over her wares.

Darlene twirled the oversized shiny key in her hands. "Seriously, Vadoma, this is really cool. It's so fancy."

"I've seen keys exactly like that one before," Vadoma said, lips pursed. "They are usually mounted on a plaque."

"Really? You've seen keys like this? It seems so unique."

"It is a key to the city, dearie."

The transistor radio started playing an old Ink Spots song, all tinny and crackling with static, a vinyl album broadcast over the airwaves, as if from far back in time.

"What do you mean, a 'key to the city'?'"

Vadoma reached for the ornamental object in Darlene's hands and took it and twirled it. Her fingernails were long and heavily lacquered. Each one had a different tiny symbol on them, a moon, a star, a sun, a pyramid, a Celtic cross.

"Villages, towns, cities occasionally give out honorary keys. They are just symbols, trophies, really, given to luminaries who are visiting or to someone who has done something generous or heroic. I think this key was an award to someone. It may have been mounted to a plaque and come loose, or it was in a fancy ornamental box that has been lost to time. Here," Vadoma said, handing the key back. "Look. Look on the bottom of the stem of the key."

Darlene took the object in her hands and held it close to her face. Engraved in the tiniest of letters on the underside of the key's stem:

City of Hollywood, California

"This is a key to Hollywood? Who do you suppose it was given to, Vadoma? This is so cool!"

Vadoma grinned. "I can't imagine they have awarded too many 'Keys to Hollywood' over the years. Just to the most special of the special, the best of the best, the crème de la crème of an entire galaxy of Hollywood stars. You know? Maybe that key belonged to Marilyn Monroe? Or perhaps Buster Keaton? Errol Flynn? Judy Garland? It belonged to one of them, or some such star. If you re-searched it, you could probably find the owner. Don't you young people use the Google to find answers to such things these days?"

Darlene smiled. "How much is it?"

Vadoma continued to place items on the tables. "I haven't priced things yet, dearie. Let me think."

"I like it, Vadoma. It speaks to me."

"It's yours, then. No charge. It's free, just for you."

"Really? But Vadoma, I want to pay for it. I think I have enough. You can't just give things away."

The old woman looked at her young friend. "Sometimes things don't belong to me. They belong to others. That key is yours, now. You take it, and run along."

Darlene held the gold key to her chest. "Thank you, Vadoma. I do love it. I love its mystery. Its aura."

Darlene placed a few paperbacks aside to buy (she secretly loved romance novels but hated hiding the fact that she adored the oft-maligned genre of "ro-mance"). She also picked out the Bakelite ring and a scratched-up birch wood ukulele, then decided she didn't have enough for them. Instead, she chose two Brenda Lee 45s. Then she stumbled upon a signed copy of Joan Didion's 1970 novel, *Play It as It Lays*. Darlene opened it to the copyright page. It was a first edition.

"Vadoma, this is a signed first edition. You shouldn't sell this. First edition books appreciate faster than almost any other collectible."

Vadoma, holding a set of plastic spoons from IKEA, looked up.

"Dearie, Joan lived in Malibu in the Seventies. She used to come to me for psychic readings. Such a lovely woman. I have dozens of signed books by her."

"Wow, I can't believe you gave her psychic readings!"

Darlene paid Vadoma for the items. She hugged the old woman.

"I'll see you next month!" she said.

"I always look forward to it! You are as reliable as the Perseid meteor shower, young lady, and just as bright and beautiful."

Darlene climbed on her bicycle and headed home. As she pedaled out of the driveway and down the palm tree-lined street, she rode past unoccupied sun-gleaming parked cars and their doors suddenly clicked, unlocked, and opened all by themselves.

Every car she passed, the doors opened wide.

Darlene stopped and put her feet to the pavement.

What on earth?

An elderly man, walking down the sidewalk, led by a leashed Bichon Frisé with a topiary groom, looked at the car doors that had suddenly opened, and then he glanced at Darlene.

"Weird, right?" she said, stepping on the pedals with her dandelion yellow Birkenstock sandals.

All the way home, car doors that she passed sprang open. It was actually embarrassing as pedestrians looked at her quizzically.

Darlene came to a busy intersection and stopped her bicycle. On the corner was an honest-to-goodness traditional savings and loan red-brick bank, with an ATM. She parked her bike, and, with the key in her hand, walked to the tinted front door. The bank was closed, the doors locked. Darlene was curious. She withdrew the key.

Nothing happened.

She stepped closer and waved the key in front of the doorway. To her amazement, but also confirming her suspicions, the doors unlatched and slowly opened.

The double doors to the bank were now wide open. No alarm sounded. No one there.

"Oh, my," she muttered. She looked at the key in her hand.

The thought did cross her mind. Could she walk in and wave the key in front of the safe?

She stared into the darkened bank. For moments, she stood there. She was tempted, ever so slightly. Thinking of everything she could buy that made her feel life's bigness. The items she just held at Vadoma's yard sale. All those beautiful things with such history! Everything in the world. She looked at the key and turned it over and over. She stood there for an eternity. Then she turned, climbed on her bike, and pedaled off.

She biked toward her west Los Angeles home, thinking very carefully about what this all meant. When she approached her front door and took out the key, the door silently swung inward. Her parents were both at work, special effects makeup artists in the movie industry working long hours on a current production about deep-sea creatures.

Darlene went to her bedroom. She put on one of the Brenda Lee records she had just bought on her old vinyl player. Her room was filled with pastel colors and yard sale treasures tucked in corners, crowded on book cases, scattered on her desk, high and low. She twirled the key in her hands, and then decided to open her window with it. Outside, the eucalyptus trees in the back yard rustled.

I could go anywhere with this key.

She could have taken all the money at that bank today. She could walk into any shop she wanted to. She could enter any house. She thought of all the possibilities.

For hours, Darlene listened to her music, doodling in her journal, reading the Joan Didion novel. In between, she thought about possessing a key that would seemingly open any door. She would only use it for good.

As the sun sank and the light in her bedroom shifted and grew darker and Brenda Lee sang, Darlene rose from her bed, where she had burrowed under her soft floral comforter.

Another Joan Didion book sat on her shelf. She had forgotten about it and now flipped through it, looking at some of the notes the previous owner had made in the margins. One page was underlined and starred: "Was there ever in anyone's life span a point free in time, devoid of memory, a night when choice was any more than the sum of all the choices gone before?"

She put on her blue jean jacket adorned with patches of peace signs and flowers and then grabbed the golden key. She was back on her bicycle before she knew it.

As she rode down L.A. side streets, doors on the parked cars opened in the hush of twilight. She passed an armored car along a curb in Santa Monica and its rear door quietly opened up.

She kept pedaling until she reached the ocean. The sun was setting into the Pacific, orange over the water. She parked her bike and, kicking off her sandals, walked across the sand, feeling the warmth of the day on the soles of her feet. The waves came in; seagulls and sand pipers skittered about. The beach was mostly empty, with a few kids, their pant legs rolled up, still splashing in the water. Down a ways, a man flew a kite.

Darlene walked up to the water, the foam of the waves kissing her feet. She held the key in her fist. She thought about it for a moment. Could she give the key to someone who really needed it? Perhaps someone who was hungry on the streets? Or someone who needed medicine but couldn't afford it? Or someone who has had no luck at all in life.

"With great power comes great responsibility," she said aloud, echoing the timeless words of one Peter Parker.

She pondered this for a long while. Some doors are meant to stay shut.

Darlene reared back, her arm cocked like a great Dodgers outfielder.

She hurled the key as far out into the ocean as possible. The golden object arched up, turning end over end, almost in slow motion. The kids down the shore were laughing as they splashed and splashed; the man's kite fluttered in the wind. The waves continued to crash. The key kept going, tumbling, windmilling, turning and then, finally, it began its downward arc towards the water.

And with a quiet splash, it disappeared into the Pacific. Sinking down, down, and, at last, landing gently on the sandy ocean floor.

Darlene stood for a moment and then turned and went back to her bicycle. She rode home to her records and her books and her bed.

~~~

Many months later, on an early summer morning as the lifeguards were just beginning to open the stations and prep the beach for the day, Vadoma swept her metal detector over the sand back and forth, back and forth. Suddenly the signal went off, loud and strong. She had found something, solid metal and heavy.

Eleven Messages from the Beyond to the Producers of
Ghost Investigators on A&E

1/ That moving rocking chair in the corner of the basement you just filmed with your grainy night vision camera? Good God! We are condemned to an eternity of purgatory. You think we want to sit in rocking chairs for a hundred million years of monotony? We prefer the oversized comfort roll armchair from Pottery Barn with optional matching tufted ottoman. Attractive and cozy!

2/ Production advice: Oversized comfort chairs can't be easily manipulated with heavy-gage clear nylon fishing line. Try heavy-gauge monofilaments or braided lines for best results.

3/ Why do paranormal investigators always look for spirits at night and in the dark? You assholes come in to our space and run around and yell and complain that the temperature just dropped precipitously. You think ghosts aren't morning people, too? The night in the haunted house scenario is so 2005.

4/ Your crews. Really. Such clichés. The portly guy wearing the *Metallica* shirt? The proliferation of trucker hats and hipster facial hair? Enough of the white guys. This is not *Duck Dynasty*. We have more SOC (spirits of color) in our realm than you have POC in yours. Get. With. The. Times!

5/ Electronic Voice Phenomena (EVP) recorders. Electromagnetic Field

(EMF) sensors. Where do you guys buy all this shit? Best Buy no longer sells music but they sell questionable paranormal electronic equipment?

6/ You ever thought of just bringing us a few venti cups of Starbucks Pikes Place or even a couple of barbacoa bowls from Chipotle? We would come out right away and with gratitude.

7/ Those green eyes your host has when you film with a night vision camera? Stop. Please. You are creeping us out.

8/ You say, "Something just touched me!" Stop that. We are not gropers. We are ghosts.

9/ If you really proved, without hesitation, the existence of the afterworld, do you really have to air this science-altering, spiritual-altering, monumental human discovery right after a rerun of *Here Comes Honey Boo Boo* or *Keeping Up with the Kardashians*?

10/ Hi. My name is Bob. I was just a normal guy in life. I worked in middle management. And now I'm just a normal spirit in the afterlife. Average. I'm average. Other ghosts say I'm actually kind of boring. And this is my point. Not all ghosts are children who died tragically in fires, or celebrity starlets wandering their historic Beverly Hills mansions. Sure, Abraham Lincoln did haunt the White House and he *did* encounter Winston Churchill in the bathroom. But President Lincoln immediately left the White House in 2017 when Trump moved in.

11/ There are billions of homo sapiens who have been born, lived, and died since our moronic species first walked the Earth. You come to a historic inn with a tragic past or an infamous murder house, and you expect us to just come out and converse? Don't fuck with us. There are far more of us than there are of you.

The Peephole

I lived in a massive apartment complex in the Bronx. There was a peephole in the front door of my apartment. When I was bored, or high on weed, I used to stare out for long expanses of time. I'd wait for all the warped people to walk past. Old ladies and their weird adult sons who lived with them, latch-key kids who came home alone after school, kids in gangs, hookers in high heels wandering the hall after midnight. All kinds of people out there, beyond the door.

The hallway beyond the little scratched convex lens was distorted, elongated, like out of a surrealist painting. I could see the stretch of dark carpet, going off in each direction. I could see the stains on the walls, and the door directly across from my unit. The door to 20E.

The hallway was long, with an insect hum of caged fluorescent lights. There were twenty-six apartments on every floor. I lived in a moderate-income public housing high-rise. They were all the same, twenty stories tall, made of concrete. The buildings were built close to each other, making the sprawling project seem like a city within a city. Unofficially, the housing development was known as "Concrete City."

It was 1974, my first year in New York. I worked at the Sam Ash music store in Manhattan most days and at nights performed with my band, Luxury. We were a new wave/punk five-piece. We mostly played shitholes out on Long Island and cockroach farms in the Village. Recently, we'd landed a few gigs at

CBGB, opening for Blondie, Talking Heads, and some others. It felt like maybe our star was on the rise.

Anyway, 20E, the unit across the hall from mine, was vacant the first year I lived in Concrete City. I never once saw anyone go in or out. Never. Then, one winter afternoon, when the sky was all gray, you know, when it starts getting dark right after fucking lunch, I was sitting on my sofa watching a game show and strumming my telecaster when I heard keys jangling in the hall. At my front door, I pressed my eye to the peephole, just in time to see the door across the way, the door to 20E, closing shut. Someone had entered the vacant unit.

The next day, while in the lobby, I made a point to look at the mailbox for 20E. The steel mailboxes were set into the wall, and someone had taped a plastic strip made with one of those label dispensers. The adhesive label read, in raised white letters: "A. Mallus."

Over the next few weeks, I heard the door to 20E open and close often. But each time I ran to the peephole, the door was either closing shut or had already closed. Once, late at night, I heard the door opening. Setting my guitar down, I rushed over to look. Down the dimly lit hallway, I saw a figure walking away, a man with a cleanshaven head. He wore a black leather jacket.

I'm not sure why I was so interested in who had moved in to 20E. Maybe I just wanted to know who my new neighbor was. But I doubt that. I didn't know my other neighbors. Sure, if I was throwing a party or had turned up my amplifier and was playing my guitar too loud, too late, I'd get the inevitable "shut the fuck up!" or the "turn that shit down!" but that was usually it. My neighbors were nothing more than angry voices in the night, mad coyotes, or they were distended strangers pacing the hall beyond the peephole. Anonymity was a way of life in Concrete City. You could get sucked into that place and no one knew who you were and no one fucking cared. If you just vanished, just up and disappeared, dead in a gutter or stuffed in the trunk of someone's car, no one would ever notice.

The only person I knew by name at Concrete City was Hennan, the security guard who sat at a half-circle command desk in the lobby. Hennan loved wearing his blue private security uniform, starched and pressed. It gave him an authority I imagined he never had before. He was probably that kid who got kicked around on the playground when he was little. But in the world of the anonymous, everyone knew Hennan because you had to walk past him to get on the elevators.

I was on my way to a show at Max's Kansas City one night when I took the elevator down to the cold lobby and walked up to Hennan.

"What's up, Nick?" he asked, one side of his mouth moving up into a smile. That was weird. He rarely smiled. Hennan had this distracting chalazion on his left eyelid, a floppy, infected sack from a clogged tear duct. I never knew anyone to have an infection for so fucking long.

I leaned on the high front of his command desk. He put a piece of blank paper over something, a magazine. It was obscured, but I could still see a part of it. Some sort of fetish porn, probably.

"Say, man, do you know who moved into 20E? That place has been, like, vacant forever. Seems like I have a new neighbor."

"Beats the fuck out of me," he said, shrugging his round shoulders like a big sack of fertilizer being loaded onto a flatbed. "Is there a problem?"

"No. I've just been wondering who moved in. That's all."

On the wall behind Hennan's desk was a bank of black-and-white closed-circuit TVs. They flicked periodically to different views around the building. I noticed one—an image of an elevator car. The camera was positioned high in the corner, looking down. In the elevator, a man was staring up at the numbers above the doors. He was wearing a black leather jacket. His head was shaved perfectly smooth. It was the man I had seen leaving 20E.

I turned and looked behind me. The lights above the six elevators indicated where each car was. Three were stopped on higher floors. Two were heading up. One was coming down. I walked over to the elevator.

Five. Four. Three. Two. One.

The brushed metal doors whisked open. But the car was empty. No one emerged. The bald guy had been on another elevator. Maybe going up.

~~~

I played a gig at CBGB that night. Afterward, Chris Stein and Debbie Harry from Blondie came back to my place to hang out. I liked them. They were cool. Most of us in the scene knew each other pretty well. It was two in the morning when we got back. We all sat on the sofa and drank beer. Chris put on some acid jazz records from my collection. After placing the stylus down on the vinyl, he walked over to the window and looked out at the faraway stream of headlights on the parkway.

"What the fuck do you do around here when you're not working?" he asked. "Doesn't seem like there's much neighborhood to walk around."

"Alexander's isn't too far from here. They have a pretty good music section," I said. "I go there sometimes. But most of the time I stay in, you know, watch TV, play guitar, write tunes. I stare out my peephole a lot, too."

"You do what?" asked Debbie. She had that towel-tousled blonde hair and cool air about her. Chris was a lucky motherfucker. He knew it.

"I stare out my peephole."

"What the fuck for?" Chris asked, taking a swig of beer.

"I don't know. It's just turned into a weird pastime for me. It's like a little fish-eye lens into another world."

"But it's not another world, man," said Chris. "It's just the fucking hallway on the other side of the door."

"Are you a voyeur?" Debbie stood and straightened her tight black and white striped skirt. She went over to the door and looked through the peephole.

"Jesus fucking Christ!" she said.

"What?" Chris and I said at the same time.

"What the fuck is that guy doing?"

"What is it?" I said, standing.

Debbie whispered, "That dude is dragging something heavy in a canvas sack. It's like there's a body in there or something. That's fucked up."

"Let me look!"

But Debbie kept her monopoly on the peephole. "Whatever he has, it's heavy, man."

"Come on! Let me see."

But Debbie kept her position.

I could hear the sounds of keys and a door unlocking, then opening. Debbie kept staring.

"That dude gives me the creeps."

She stepped back, giving me enough room to lean into the peephole. The door to 20E was closing shut.

"What did you see?"

"This dude, with, like, the meanest face ever. His head was shaved. Piercings in his ears. He was dragging this army green sack down the hall. Whatever the hell was in it, it was heavy, man. The sack was tied shut at one end. Who the fuck is that guy, anyway?"

"I don't know. He moved in a few weeks ago but I haven't met him. I've only seen glimpses of the dude."

"What else goes on outside that peephole?" Chris asked, walking to the door. I stepped away and he looked out. The hall was quiet. Lifeless.

"All sorts of shit," I said. "If you stand there long enough and look out, you'll see all kinds of stuff."

A couple of weeks passed. My band was playing more gigs than ever. A couple of record label execs had come to a few shows. There was a buzz to the whole scene at that time. Between band practice, gigs, and my day job, I hadn't been around Concrete City much, except to crash. One winter afternoon I came home. I walked down the long hall to my apartment unit. I fished the keys out of my coat pocket as I approached my door. It was then that I noticed it. The door to 20E was halfway open. A wedge of light spilled out. I looked at the keys in my hand and found the one to unlock my door. I looked at the doorway of 20E again. What the hell? I crossed the hall and stuck my head into the apartment, just a little ways.

"Hello?"

No answer.

With my thumb and forefinger, I knocked, using the scratched, faux brass knocker. No response. I pushed the door wider to get a better look inside. Acid jazz playing on a record player.

"Hello?" I called again. "I think you left your door open."

The front door opened into the living room. The floor plan was similar to mine. The place was immaculate (opposite of mine). There was a fuzzy love seat and a coffee table with lit candles on it. Behind it was a large window with a view of the other concrete buildings. A tall wooden shelf held hundreds and hundreds of vinyl records. In the dining room, there was a small round table set with more lit candles, two place settings, and two chairs. And I could even see a bit of the kitchen, everything in order, the fridge was humming and the knives all in a neat row in the block.

"Hello?" I called again. "Your door was open. I can close it for you."

On the floor, by the sofa, I spotted something, dark and furry. An animal? I stepped into the apartment. What the hell was that thing? I couldn't tell. It was a clump of dark hair or something. A wig? I took another step, closer to that thing on the floor. I squinted. I was sure it was a wig.

A clearing of the throat at the door. My heart lurched in my chest, like a car going over a speed bump repeatedly.

"You Alex?" said a woman.

I turned. She was in silhouette but I couldn't make out her hair in the light—brown or black, I couldn't tell. She was curvy. Very round hips and big breasts.

"I'm sorry?" I said.

"Are you Alex?" she said again. Impatient. "The clock's ticking."

I moved towards her, closer to the door.

"No. No, I'm not. Sorry. I think the guy here left his door open. I just came in to let him know."

"He probably left it open for me."

As I stepped closer, I could see her better. Her purple shiny spandex pants and a black tube top were skin tight. Her belly sagged out over her waist just a bit. Her hair was dyed. Or was it a wig? Her lips were slathered in a wet gloss. She was much taller than me in her platform shoes. She was clutching a purse with a gold chain for a strap. I could smell her, too. She smelled like a Charms Blow Pop.

"Well, where's Alex?" she said.

"No idea."

"Really?" she said, looking me up and down. "You looking for anything? I could make you very happy."

"No, no. That's cool. I mean, that sounds nice and all, but I gotta roll."

I moved around her, to the door.

"Come on, sugar. There must be something you need. We all got our things. You wanna be tied up? That's cool. You like to role play? That's cool, too. You like to watch? Whatever you want. Come on."

I have to admit, it almost sounded thrilling. But I just wanted to get out of 20E.

"I'm sorry."

"You don't know what you're missing."

"No. I just need to leave."

And I stepped out, into the fluorescent-lit hallway. She stood in the doorway, looking at me. I didn't want her to see that I lived just across the hall, so I left. I took the elevator down. When the doors whisked open in the lobby, I saw Hennan sitting there, reading. He again hid whatever it was he was looking at and looked up.

"Hey, Nick. Everything cool?"

"Yeah. Yeah, it's fine. Just checking my mail."

I walked over to the postal boxes and checked mine, even though I'd already done so earlier. I waited a bit longer and then went back to the elevator.

"Night," said Hennan, flipping something over.

"Night," I said, as the doors shut and I rode back up. I made my way down the still hallway to my apartment. To my relief, she was gone. And the door to 20E was closed.

I went to bed. But in the middle of the night, I woke to the sound of a scream. A woman. A single, terrified, scream. There were all kinds of sounds in Concrete City at all hours of the day. I rolled over and drifted back to sleep.

I had the next day off from work. Luxury had been gigging so damned often I just needed a break. I sprawled out on my couch and read some Bukowski. A few pages in, I heard a door open and shut. I put the book down and went to the peephole. I leaned up against the lens. Weird. It was dark. I couldn't see out. I moved back a step, wet my thumb with my tongue, and cleaned the lens with a circular motion. I leaned into it again. It was still dark. But not completely black—dusky. Like when you close your eyes and there is a light on. There's that blood-colored darkness as you look through your eyelids.

Suddenly, the peephole shined with light. I blinked several times, and when I focused again, I saw it was the bald guy from across the way, from 20E. He had been holding his thumb up to the peephole. When he lowered his hand, I saw him. He had on an army green jacket. His ears had multiple silver hoops.

He sneered at the lens. At me. He knew that I heard his door. He knew I was looking out. He was fucking with me.

I jumped back. Sat down on the sofa. Tried to forgot about that guy. I regretted ever looking out that peephole. I watched TV. Played guitar. Popped a couple beers. Smoked a joint.

The following week my band had a gig at Club 82, a popular venue in the basement of a building in the Village. We had never performed there before. The Dolls had played there. Bowie hung out there. So did Lou Reed. It was sort of the epicenter for the glam scene, mainly because the club was known as a hangout for drag queens. It was during our opening song, "Just Another Face Staring out Another Window," I saw a dude in drag looking at me. He held a bottle of beer at his waist, the way a blue-collar guy does. He wore a dark dress and a dark wig. His lipstick was dark, too. He had a large leather purse slung over his shoulder. And he just stared. He didn't look at anyone else in the band. Just me. It was disconcerting as fuck. Throughout the song, I kept looking up at him and his eyes were fixed. He brushed his wig back a little and it was then that I saw multiple earrings shimmer in the bar neon. It was the guy from 20E.

After that, the gig was brutal. The dude never once took his eyes off me. I fucked up several times on several songs. My band mates were not happy. I couldn't get off that stage fast enough after the gig. I packed up my guitar and bailed. I apologized to the guys for my mistakes.

"Too much on my mind," I said. "Sorry. It won't happen again."

I worked my way through the crowd to the front door. I had lost sight of the guy from 20E and I hoped he had lost sight of me. I took the stairs two at a time and exited out onto East 4th Street. The fresh night air came as a relief. It was late, but the East Village was bustling with people, gay and straight couples walking arm in arm, panhandlers on the corners, a guy puking in a wire-mesh trashcan.

My guitar case in hand, I walked to the subway, occasionally glancing over my shoulder to see if I was being followed. I didn't see the guy. I moved down the subway. I don't know why, but it just felt like I was being followed. I kept turning around, yet no one was there. When I reached the platform, I could see the light of the train far down the tunnel. Then, at the top of the staircase, I heard the clicking of high heels. Someone was coming.

I could hear the train rushing towards me. The heels were also getting closer. Methodically coming down the steps. Closer. Closer.

The train whisked into the station. The doors glided open and I stepped on. I waited for the doors to close, but they remained open. *Come on, dammit. Close.*

Finally, they shut. No one else stepped on. The train moved forward. I wondered if whoever it was coming down the stairway had stepped on to another subway car.

I thought about the guy from 20E. Standing outside my front door, knowing I was looking out. I thought about him at Club 82, laser-focused only on me. It was crazy. I was rushing to get home, to Concrete City, yet he knew where I lived. He was just across the hall. I couldn't get away from him. And I still had a creeping feeling he was on the train, on another car. I decided to get off a stop early. If he was on the subway, he wouldn't expect that.

It was late and I had a good six blocks to walk. And unlike the East Village, when I got off the train, the Bronx was quiet and desolate. The liquor stores and corner grocers were all gated up. A few cars were still out cruising, a few gang kids here and there, a few derelicts, but that was it. I could hear sirens. Lights twinkled in the high rises. I walked quickly, peering over my shoulder to see if I was being followed. Nothing. No one was behind me. But it felt like someone was.

I rounded a corner. Was I just imagining things? Was I being paranoid? Maybe the dude in drag at the show wasn't the guy from 20E. Maybe my mind was just playing tricks. I just wanted to get back to my own place, behind the security of my locked door. Then I heard the clicking of high heels behind me, from around the corner I had just turned.

I was close. I could see Concrete City rising up like a filthy mirage of cement and light. I just had to cross a long vacant lot of rubble, weeds, and discarded bottles of booze. I hurried, and it felt like a football field that I was crossing. I was hesitant to look over my shoulder. Nervous. Was he trailing me? Another empty bottle of gin. A dirty, stuffed animal with its tail missing. Broken bits of cinderblock. A used rubber. I picked up my pace to a trot. I was halfway across the field. A gun shot fired off, far, far away. Three-quarters across the field. Closer to the safety of my apartment and my locked door. I turned and looked, finally.

And there he was. Just beginning the trek across the vacant lot. The man from 20E. He reached into his purse and withdrew something, even as he ventured out on the vacant blighted stretch. The object in his hand gleamed under the city lights. It was a large kitchen knife.

I ran. I stepped onto the drive that lead up to Concrete City. I ran as fast as I could. Past the first three buildings, until I reached my high-rise. I pushed the glass door open. Hennan was behind his desk.

"Hey, Nick," he said, placing his hands over the pages of the magazine on his desk.

"Hey," I huffed. I walked across the lobby. Pressed hard on the elevator button, looking up at the lights over the doors. There was a car coming down. Five. Four. Three.

It stopped at two.

I looked behind me. The guy still hadn't come into the building. It was dark outside and I couldn't see much beyond the doors.

The elevator started moving again. Two. One.

The doors opened. An old lady with a bulky bag stepped off. I hurried in and pressed the button for my floor.

Looking out, beyond the glass door, he emerged from the darkness. The door of the building opened and there he was, the guy in the dress, the high heels, and the greasy dark wig, clutching a kitchen knife. He glared at me from across the lobby.

I jabbed at the "door close" button on the elevator panel.

He moved across the lobby, in my direction.

Hennan sat there, deep in his magazine. Then the guy made a noise, or I did, and Hennan looked up, saw him, saw the knife, and moved from around his desk.

The elevator doors closed.

I was sweating and trembling. I had to move the fuck out of Concrete City.

I ran down the hall to my apartment with my keys in hand and I was in.

I locked the dead bolt. I latched the chain.

My hands were still trembling. I sat on the sofa and lit a joint.

Should I call the police? Should I phone down to Hennan at the security desk to see what happened?

I took a long drag of the joint. The warmth filled my lungs. I started to mellow, the tension throughout my body released.

I went to the phone to dial the police. I had just been chased by a lunatic with a long kitchen knife. But then I heard sirens drawing closer and closer to Concrete City. I stood before my living room window, with all the city and its seven million secrets out there before me. Three squad cars and an ambulance were speeding towards my building. They pulled into the circular drive, lights bouncing off all the concrete buildings. Officers rushed from their cars. The EMTs moved out of their ambulance with speed. They swung open the twin doors on the back of their vehicle and withdrew a long white stretcher. This wasn't good.

I sat on my sofa and drank. I waited for a knock on my door, from the cops, there to question me. But it never came. I wanted desperately to know what had happened in the lobby. But I didn't dare go down there. I drank myself to sleep. It was a long night.

The next morning, I took my time, making sure I looked both ways in the hall before going out there. I ran to the elevators, hit the lobby button hard.

I didn't know what I expected down there. There was an old-timer from the building standing around. I'd seen him before. He always wore a baby blue knit ski cap, loose threads poking everywhere, even on the hottest New York summer days.

"What was all the commotion about last night?" I asked, pretending that I didn't know anything.

"A big ole ruckus. Old Hennan was down here, of course. Saw a guy rush into the building with a knife," he said. When he spoke, there was a slight asthmatic whistle in his breath. "He was wearin' lady's clothing. A dress. High heels. And he had that big knife!"

"What happened?" I asked. There was not one sign of a scuffle, or wrong doing of any kind in the lobby.

"Hennan was sitting behind his desk, see," said the old-timer. "And the guy rushed in with that knife. And that's when Hennan sprang into action! Boom! We sure are lucky to have him watching over us."

"What did Hennan do?"

"He tried to stop the guy. He was after something, or someone. And Hennan got in his way. The guy didn't like it. He swung at Hennan with the knife!"

As the old-timer said this, he made the gesture of someone lunging with a blade.

"And then what happened?" I asked.

"Hennan pulled out his gun."

"And?"

"He shot him."

"Dead?"

"Dead. They still don't know what the guy was up to. It wasn't until after they had loaded him up in the ambulance and said he was gone, that they actually IDed him."

"Who was he?" I asked.

"He actually lived in this building!" said the old-timer. "Right here, in 20E."

"Really?"

The cops never came to question me. *That* surprised me. I guess the police see so many freakish things every night of the year, they just closed the book right away.

Hennan was back a few days later, at his desk, reading whatever it was he read. His left hand was bandaged. I asked him how he was doing. He shrugged and went back to his reading. I'm not sure he even remembered me coming in that night.

I thought about getting the hell out of Concrete City after that. But I really couldn't afford to move. I stayed on, for another year. My band eventually broke up, which sucked since so many of our friends were signing deals with major labels. I kept working at the music store. Paying my bills. 20E stayed empty for that year. Then, one day, I heard keys in the hall. A door opening. I rushed to my own door and leaned up against it, and looked out the peephole, but no one was there.

The House They Used to Live In

While on a business trip to Chicago, Jack decided to drive by the old house. They lived there twenty-two years. How time had vanished with the slight of a magician's hand—now you see it, now you don't.

Jack crossed the threshold with his wife on their May wedding day in that house. They had welcomed their only daughter, Aiko, into it. He had built his career as a software designer right there, in that house.

Twenty-two magnificent years.

Now, Aiko was grown, off to medical school and, at present, a resident at Mayo.

The memories were good and precious and fleeting. People had always told Jack to enjoy it; be in the moment. "Kids grow up so fast," they cautioned.

There was, of course, Jack's long cage match with booze in that house. Those memories weren't so hot. They screwed up his marriage for a while. There were fights, but he and his wife eventually worked it out. He got a handle on his disease, with her support. But soon after the cancer diagnosis came, the rounds of radiation and chemo ensued. He beat one disease only to trade it in for another. But Jack beat cancer, too. He was now seven years cancer free.

As he drove to the house on Hamilton Street, it all came back. He realized, as his rental car headed north on Lake Shore Drive, that a house is like a memory vault. Everything is stored there. All of it.

It was snowing in Chicago. Big, light flakes falling down in constellations.

The snow was pelting the windshield, the wipers thumping back and forth. It was snowing out over the dark expanse of Lake Michigan, and all across the city.

Jack drove through the old neighborhood. The multicolored holiday lights were still aglow on the lamp posts and in storefront windows and on the houses. It was the week after Christmas.

He drove by the park he used to take his daughter to when she was young, the swings and the teeter totter sat still and cold in the night. He drove by the library he took Aiko to when she was child.

> *... So, gently, and using the greatest of care, the elephant stretched his great trunk through the air, and he lifted the dust speck and carried it over and placed it down, safe, on a very soft clover ...*

Jack smiled as he drove down the quiet street, past the library in darkness, the lights off for the night.

"Do you think the library mouse is there?" he heard his baby girl asking, tugging on his shirt, a long-ago memory.

Jack turned down Hamilton. It was dark and the snow continued to cascade down. The trees that lined the streets had grown since they had moved away, just as his daughter had grown. Jack wondered if any of the old neighbors were still around.

And then he reached the house, the humble red brick Georgian with the white shutters. It hadn't changed much, not much at all. He parked the car across the street, under an amber street lamp. The lights were on in the large living room window. He thought of Thanksgiving dinners and teeth under pillows with notes for the Tooth Fairy. He recalled coming back from school musicals and science fairs. Throwing the football out in the street with his little girl and taking the training wheels off her bike as she pedaled for the first time, right where he was now parked.

"I'm doing it, Daddy! I'm riding a bike!"

He thought of the Christmas tree in the living room all lit up, and the year he gave Aiko the orange Tabby, which she named "Boots" and immediately held the cat close under her chin and closed her eyes and smiled and sighed deep as the universe.

He thought about fourteen years later, digging with a spade in the hard, frozen backyard on a November day and burying Boots, Aiko, a teenager, by his side, her dark eyes filled with clear pools of tears.

That house was so filled with memories.

As Jack sat in the car, a light flipped on in an upstairs window. Aiko's old bedroom. How many nights had he rocked his baby girl in that very spot? She always had so much trouble falling asleep. He often spent an hour or more, cradling his dark-haired little baby in his arms as she sucked on her thumb, eyes closed. Jack recalled the frustrations of his little girl crying and not being able to drift off. "Sleep onset disorder," the doctor had called it. He would sing to her, and sway her back and forth, and rub his nose against hers and kiss her soft forehead. And only after he was convinced that she had finally surrendered to slumber, would he place her in her crib, and even then, she often woke the minute he set her down. For a young dad, just getting used to the routine of patience and little babies—it was all such an adjustment. Jack would get frustrated and resentful. Parenting was hard.

He sat in his car and looked at the window. What he would do to have one of those frustrating moments with his little girl again. Just one. He wouldn't be frustrated, he thought. He wouldn't be resentful. No. He would relish it. All of it.

As he looked at the house, and at the bedroom window aglow, a man appeared. Young. Dark hair. Unshaven. He moved about the room, and, then, disappeared for a moment. After a minute, he returned. He was holding a baby. He started to sway back and forth, back and forth looking down at the child in his arms.

Jack sat out on the street in his rental car and watched. He felt guilty at first, watching the father and child this way. Then he felt envy. What he would do for just one more moment in that room again with his own child.

Why was I always in such a hurry? Why was I so impatient?

The man continued to rock the baby, doing his best to help the little child drift off. The dance between father and baby went on for ten minutes, Jack watching outside from his car, the snow still falling.

The father rubbed his nose against his infant's face. He kissed the baby's forehead. Jack couldn't believe the similarities to his own memories.

That was me, all those years ago.

And upstairs, in the bedroom, the young father was tired. His baby wouldn't drift off. It was this way often. People said she needed to be "sleep trained." To just set her down in the crib and let her cry it out. But he had brought that baby into this world and he took a solemn pledge to protect her. He couldn't stand listening to her wail, wondering where her daddy had gone and why he wasn't coming to her aid.

So night after night he rocked her to sleep and sometimes it felt like it took forever. And that night, while he was rocking that little child, he moved towards the window and looked out. Snow was coming down, sleepy and silver, each flake infinite in its intricacy. Holding his daughter in his arms, he pressed closer to the window pane.

A car was parked outside, under the sulphur street lamp. The engine was idling, exhaust expelling blue-gray clouds from the tailpipe.

The father squinted. It was odd. Through the dark and the falling snow, he swore, the man sitting behind the wheel of that car—he was looking up, right at him.

Weird

My little brother is weird. In fact, I call him this. "Weird." It has become his nickname. His real name is Edwin.

It started when he was little. The weirdness. When he was seven and got his first library card he went to the movie section and wandered around until he found something he wanted to check out. It was the movie *Harold and Maude*. I'd never seen it. It was, like, one of those old time, golden-era Hollywood films from 1971 or something.

"What is that?" I asked, taking the DVD out of his little hands. I read the back. The movie was about some teenage kid who has this sort of creepy relationship with a grandma or something. The kid was bizarre, morose, a Goth, I suppose.

"You can't check that crap out," I told Edwin. "It's not age appropriate."

That's when Edwin freaked out and had a tantrum. I hated it when Edwin had tantrums. His meltdowns were epic. Right there, in the Goodman Library, in the movie section, his face contorted like a wax figure melting and his eyes filled with tears. He opened his mouth. I knew he was getting ready to scream. When a kid has a tantrum and they open their mouth but nothing comes out, you know it's going to be terrible. Edwin was breathing in. Filling his lungs so he could let out a scream louder than a tornado siren.

"Chill out, Edwin," I told him. "There's like a million other DVDs, man.

Here," I said, quickly grabbing a DVD off the shelf. *The Godfather II.* "This is perfect. Check this one out."

But Edwin went and screamed anyway. And it was worse than terrible. And then he did this little routine, something he didn't do very often, he collapsed on the carpeted floor and started to kick with his left leg so he was doing circles. And he kept screaming. People around the library looked at us. One stack over, through the gap in the shelf, a pair of eyes glared at me. Someone said, "Shhhhh." Such a library cliché.

Edwin kept spinning on the burlap grey carpet, kicking his foot like a bicyclist pushing off the ground to gain momentum.

"Okay! Okay! You can check the movie out!" I said. "Just shut the hell up."

And he took *Harold and Maude* home and that's when it all started.

~~~

Harold and Maude is about a creepy introverted guy who hangs out at funerals and fakes his own suicides and stuff. He drives a hearse he converted from a vintage Jaguar. The kid in the story meets this old lady at a funeral and they forge this sort of eccentric relationship. The old lady teaches the kid all about life and crap. They have this sort of creepy romantic bond, too.

Weird watched that movie like a dozen times in a week. He'd sit on the couch in our living room, the curtains all drawn, staring blankly, bathed in the blue glow of the TV. When the movie would end, he would just hit "play" again. Mom worked at the Wal-Mart during the days and Dad was an electrician. I was eleven, and they put me in charge. So I let Weird watch that movie over and over again. One time, Dad came home and saw Weird sitting on the couch staring at the TV. Weird was sitting upside down, trying to do a handstand on the sofa. His lips were mouthing the lines of the movie.

"What is this garbage you're watching, Edwin?"

Weird didn't answer. He just kept looking at the television in a trance.

Dad clomped over in his heavy work boots and turned the television off.

Weird had a meltdown. His face turned all rubber and he started screaming.

"Shut the hell up! Go play a video game! Do something that uses your imagination!"

Weird stomped off to our bedroom crying.

A few days later, Weird figured out how to download *Harold and Maude* on the computer. He was tech-savvy for a seven-year-old. He continued to watch that film over and over. And that's when he got into other gothic stuff. When he wasn't watching *Harold and Maude*, he watched old episodes of *The Addams Family*. I took him to the library and he found a book of cartoons by Edward Gorey and he stared at them all the time, too. Weird would leave his own primitive doodles all over the house, freaky pen and ink sketches of birds eating human brains and drawings of skeletons all gathered around tables for Thanksgiving dinner eating a skeleton turkey. I have to admit, the kid was a good artist.

One hot summer day he begged me to take him to a vintage store downtown. He took all the change out of the old coffee can on the dresser. He counted it out on the floor. He had $19.18 in there. He also had a twenty-dollar bill that grandma had given him for his last birthday. The bill still smelled like granny.

It was a gray winter day and we walked downtown to the Goodwill store and Edwin shopped around with great focus.

"What are you looking for?" I asked him.

He didn't say anything. More and more he was silent and sullen and weird.

He walked around the resale shop looking for God knows what. He rounded a rack of mangy wool women's coats—real old lady stuff—when he walked up to a girl his age, standing there between baby doll dresses and cardigan sweaters that smelled of perfume. It was odd. She had long black hair, wore horn-rimmed glasses, and had on all black. I didn't know Goths came in such small packages. Edwin and the girl looked at each other for a moment and, after a while, she smiled. It was sweet, I suppose. Weird just nodded at her and then she walked off. When she walked away, Weird turned and watched her for the longest time. The little gothic girl found a lady, probably her mom, and grabbed her hand. They left the store soon after that. Weird watched them as they walked out. The girl turned and looked in through the glass doors and waved at Weird. He waved back.

Weird piled his arms up with clothes and a long, heavy double-breasted suede coat that had dirty sheepskin lapels. He had found three super-wide paisley grandpa ties and some old corduroy pants.

He paid with grandma's twenty and counted off the rest of the total in change on the counter of the Goodwill.

The clothes didn't fit him so well, but Weird didn't care. He tried them on anyway and looked at himself in the long mirror in our parents' room. He was swimming in that ratty shit.

"Those clothes need to be fumigated," I told him.

He just looked at me standing over him in my Nirvana T-shirt and ripped blue jeans. More and more, we were becoming total opposites. I didn't have much in common with my little brother any more. No one did.

~~~

Years went by and Weird got weirder. He was quiet most of the time. He spoke some at school, I guess, and the teachers always complimented him on his report cards for being "the quiet, imaginative kind." He did well in English class, always carting around a copy of Poe's *Tales of Mystery and Imagination*. He loved Ambrose Bierce, too.

He cut his black hair into this stupid bowl cut. He sort of looked like Mr.

Spock. One day in fifth grade he wore a little gray tweed schoolboy uniform to his class—the ones with the shorts and the matching little jacket. He had on dark socks and dark shoes.

"What are you, Angus Young from AC/DC?" I asked.

He just stared at me and then walked off.

Mom and Dad dismissed Weird. They didn't pay much attention to him.

"He's a lost cause," Dad would say. "Something ain't right with that boy. Brooke, do you think he's turning into your cousin from San Francisco?"

Mom shrugged.

By the eighth grade, Weird had sprouted. He was tall for his age. Gangly. He finally fit all those clothes he had bought at the Goodwill, years back. He started wearing them to school every day. He loved those wide ties and that heavy suede coat. He still watched *Harold and Maude*, and he doodled constantly in his school notebooks, creepy macabre drawings of skeleton children picking daisies and stuff.

One day while Weird was in the eighth grade, a kid in his class, Malcolm Horner, committed suicide. I never met Malcolm, but everyone in town was talking about it. The kid had found his grandfather's shotgun in the garage. They said you could hear the sound of his Rottweiler out in the yard crying like a baby after the gun blast.

The day after Malcolm killed himself, his desk at school sat empty. Weird sat behind Malcolm. The biology teacher, Mr. Cooper, told Weird to move up. I had Mr. Cooper, when I was younger. He wore a terrible toupee and always complained about his psoriasis.

"Edwin," said Mr. Copper. "Why don't you move up to Malcolm's seat? He won't be needing it any longer."

The reason I know about this is because Edwin told me about it. It's the most he had said to me in years. We were lying in our twin beds with the lights out. Dad had burnt something in the oven, some sort of meat, and the whole house smelled.

"Davie, why did Malcolm Horner kill himself?" Edwin asked me, both of us in bed, under covers, in the cobalt darkness.

"I don't know, Edwin," I said. "I don't know."

I could see Edwin lying there, staring straight up at the ceiling, his chest rising up and down.

"There's a new kid in my grade. She moved from across town. She didn't know Malcolm. I wish she could sit there. I don't want to sit in that chair," he said.

"Ask her to switch seats. Ask any of the kids."

"No one wants to sit there."

"Sorry, Edwin. I know it sucks. I'm sorry. I really am."

~~~

As a freshman in high school, Weird had more freedom. After dinner he would go out a lot. Mom and Dad never asked where he was going. He was a good kid in some ways. He would finish everything on his plate, carry the dishes to the sink, wash them, put them in the rack, and then he would leave.

"Be careful," Mom always said.

Weird would grin, slightly, and nod.

When Weird was fifteen, I was nineteen. I was attending the local vocational school to study computers. I still lived at home. Weird went out after dinner most nights and, for some reason, one October evening, I decided to follow him. I mean, where does someone like that go every night?

It was a windy evening, brittle autumn leaves kicked up in dervishes as I followed Weird, making sure to keep my distance. He had on his long brown overcoat with the sheepskin lapels, the collar turned up. His hands were delved deep into his pant pockets. Weird walked down the sidewalk, making sure to step on every crack as he always did. The tree-lined street was dark, save for a few street lamps bucketing up and down in the wind. The swaying lights cast elongated, living shadows, like the way an illuminated swimming pool looks at night when someone jumps in the water.

I followed Weird for at least twenty minutes, as he walked through downtown, past the bookstore, underneath the movie theater marquee, and by the old Carnegie library. He kept on going until he reached Third Street. Where was he going? To someone's house, I wondered? He didn't have any friends. I mean, nobody wanted to be around Weird.

The streets were quiet. The bell in the Sacred Heart Church tower, a half mile away, tolled seven. Weird turned down Third Street and then I realized where he was headed.

The cemetery.

At the end of Third Street were the open iron gates, one of them barely hanging by its hinge. Weird walked into the graveyard and kept on going into the field of headstones and mausoleums.

I remained a good distance behind my brother. While he no longer had tantrums, I knew that he would be pissed at me for following him. My brother had no friends and he loved to be alone. He was also very private about his weirdness and didn't take kindly to questions about his ways. I often wondered if he was going to grow up to be the next Lee Harvey Oswald.

Granite headstones surrounded me. Some were very old, dating back to before the Civil War. There were graves marked for people who had lived more than one hundred years, there were graves for babies who had lived just days. I walked past one small headstone and there was a dirty teddy bear leaning up against it. It had been sitting there, leaning against the grave for weeks, it seemed.

Weird walked around a tall statue of an angel, her wings outstretched, and he moved down a slope. The wind was really whipping up, leaves stirring and swirling.

I walked past a headstone with a jack-o-lantern and a full bottle of beer placed next to it.

I ventured around the angel statue and down the hillside. Weird was well in front of me. And then I noticed, someone was there at the back of the cemetery, near the iron fence. A slight figure in shadow. Weird walked up to the person.

I stopped and looked on.

It was a woman, or a girl. She was petite. She had on a long vintage trench coat and her long black hair lifted slightly in the wind. Moonlight glinted off her spectacles.

Weird reached out with both hands and she took them.

I moved closer.

She had a blanket spread out on the ground and a basket that she opened. She pulled out two candles and lit them.

And then Weird did something completely unlike him. He kissed her. And she smiled after their lips had parted.

And then I realized. It was the little gothic girl from all those years ago. The Goth from the Goodwill shop. She was all grown up.

And she was, apparently, with Weird.

They kissed again, softly.

And as I stood there, in the cemetery, the wind whipping up all around me, I thought to myself: there really is someone out there for everyone, no matter how weird they are.

The Shadows Behind the Trees

For several years, the family traveled to Lake Wanagi for late summer vacations. They stayed at the old Edgerton resort, in one of eight rustic cabins on the water, surrounded by the dense wall of pine that went on for a hundred miles in every direction. Loons cried out in the darkness of morning. When the white-gold sun lifted above the fringe of the conifers, the lake water glimmered with incandescent static. The days were warm, the nights chilly, perfect for woolen sweaters and bonfires down by the lake. The fires were the most magical, especially when the family's only son, Thomas, was young—the warm orange glow, the smell of cinder, the pop of wet wood. Shadows played. Elongated midnight Kokopellis dancing along the walls of the surrounding woods.

Chris and Cindy Tucker knew there wouldn't be many more of these family outings. After all, Thomas was eighteen and had just started his studies in biology—Cornell called with a full scholarship.

As the family drove north in the minivan, no one said a thing about this being the last trip, the very last, but there was the unspoken sense of it. Chris listened to Chet Baker over the car stereo, his left hand draped over the steering wheel, his fingers tapping to the rhythm of the cool jazz. Chris Tucker was a bit of a throwback, with his short-sleeved Sears and Roebuck sports shirt, Timex flexband watch, and thick head of brown Vitalis hair with graying temples.

Cindy Tucker, her hair pulled back into a neat ponytail, looked from behind large sunglasses out at the passing scenery and then glanced down to her e-reader and the story of *Tess of the D'Urbervilles*.

They were young parents to have a child entering adulthood. Cindy and Chris were just forty.

They arrived at twilight. The minivan turned off the old rural highway and down the two-mile gravel lane that led through the thick forest to the lodge. Rocks and pebbles crunched beneath the tires. With the sun now behind the woods, the land was awash in evergreen. The van passed by a large, weathered wooden sign along the shoulder:

Edgerton Resort: Est. 1932. Welcome Families!

The billboard for the lodge had been there for more than a half century, as evidenced by its general state of wear, and the happy, swirling, unmistakable font type of Eisenhower-era America.

Thomas looked out the window at the passing billboard.

"Do you think that sign was here when the little girl went missing in the woods?"

"I don't know, honey," Cindy answered, looking up from her e-book. "You could ask Mr. Dunn."

Mr. Dunn. The proprietor of the Edgerton Resort for as long anyone could remember. He was a round man, unshaven. He favored old caps that hid underneath a full head of powder-white hair. He ambled about with the aid of an old, wooden walking stick with the face of a Chippewa chief etched into the handle. Mr. Dunn had a hint of a brogue that was faintly Irish, faintly Canadian, faintly something else. He was outside when the family arrived, stacking wood at the water's edge. He turned and waved with his cane, as Chris Tucker parked the car outside cabin number five. The Tuckers climbed out of the minivan. The first firefly of the evening lit, then another, and another.

"Welcome, Tucker family!" called Mr. Dunn. "Welcome!"

He shook hands and gave bear hugs. "Let me help you!" he said, opening the rear door and coupling a stout hand around a suitcase handle.

The cabin was just as it always was: two small bedrooms with plump beds covered in handmade quilts; a kitchenette with a small fridge and knotty pine cabinets; a dining area with a little checkered table and four chairs, and a space up front with a sofa, two cushioned chairs, and a large bay window looking out on the lake.

After the family had unloaded and unpacked and stocked the kitchen cabinets and the refrigerator with food they had brought, they slipped into their jackets and made their way down to the lake for the bonfire. Mr. Dunn ignited the fire, a sheet of flame rising high into the night, glowing embers drifting heavenward. Thomas buttoned his jean jacket and lowered the brim of his ball cap. Mr. Dunn had set out four Adirondack chairs and was seated in one, stoking the flames with a long bough.

"This is the thirteenth year you have vacationed at the resort," he said. "Thirteen years! Can you believe it? It's become an end-of-season tradition. My Lord, it's amazing how time vanishes with the speed of a film dissolve."

Mr. Dunn looked up at Chris Tucker. "How is life in the mad sprawl of the big city, Chris? Still going a thousand-and-one miles an hour, are we? Designing and building and architecting?"

"A thousand and two," said Chris, sitting down. "Business has been good." Cindy and Thomas took seats, too.

"And how are you, Mr. Dunn?" asked Cindy, wrapping her arms around herself for warmth. The entire group was bathed in orange firelight.

"About the same. It's quiet here in the north woods at the end of the season. It gets lonely. You're the last guests, as usual. In a few weeks I'll go and board up the cabins, and bunker down like an old tired bear and hibernate until next season, God willing."

Mr. Dunn turned to Thomas, "Started school I hear?"

"Yes, sir," said Thomas. "A month ago. I came home just for this. I'll miss a few classes of course, but it's okay with my professors. I didn't want to miss out on the annual family trip." Thomas smiled. Despite his height and neatly trimmed beard, there was still a boyishness to him, a touch of wonder.

"You make your parents proud, son," said Mr. Dunn. He smiled and turned to Chris Tucker. "The bird is out of the nest. Why, I remember when you all first came to the Edgerton. Thomas was so young—just a wee one. And you both were young parents, too."

Chris smiled and nodded. Cindy looked at the fire. Thomas noticed the look on his mother's face. Chris did, too.

"Mr. Dunn?" asked Thomas. "Every year we have come here, you've told the story of that little girl. I don't know why, but when we drove up the road to the resort today, I was wondering, was that sign for the Edgerton here back then? When, you know, she went missing?"

Mr. Dunn was silent for moment, then, finally: "That was a little before my time, Thomas. But I imagine so, yes. When I bought the resort, the old owners told me that story and I've passed it along over the years, over the generations, as a warning. To caution parents and adventuresome children to take the forest very seriously. One careless moment," Mr. Dunn snapped his fingers for effect, "and you are lost forever, like that poor little girl so long, long ago."

"So that wasn't some story you made up to scare me?" asked Thomas. "So I wouldn't wander off and explore?"

"No," said Dunn, turning to the fire. "No, it wasn't. I wish it were just a tall tale. But she was real. All too real. Her name was Francine. Poor, sweet dear. Eight years old. She's up here with her family having fun, and in an instant— one click of the camera shutter, one flash of lightning, dammit—she wanders off into the woods and she's gone forever. Lost."

The family was quiet. The fire popped and more sparks flittered up into the air. Beyond the flames, the dark lake was still and eternal. On the far other side of the water, the black woods were wild.

~~~

Early the next morning, Thomas went for a hike.

"Be careful," said Cindy. "Be back by lunch."

Thomas smiled and waved and turned.

"I love you!" called Cindy.

"Love you, too!" called Thomas.

Chris Tucker stood by his wife and sipped steaming coffee from a stainless steel travel mug as they watched their child march towards a trail.

"How did our son grow up so damned fast?" asked Chris.

Cindy was quiet. She watched Thomas walk off into the forest, sunlight falling in shafts through the high treetops. He strolled through a clearing, around a bend, and out of sight.

~~~

Thomas Tucker walked for more than an hour: up hills, across stepping stones in fast rushing creeks, through clearings of wind-swept grass fields, through the endless thick of forest. He came to a high vertical bluff of Precambrian rock overlooking the lake. The wind was blowing. He stared out at the white-capped water. A bald eagle glided over the lake. Thomas had stood at this exact spot many times over the years. He knew these woods well. As he gazed out on the water, he was lost in thought.

At once, there was a sharp cracking sound behind him, a twig breaking, then, a drumbeat of footfalls running off somewhere into the woods. Thomas turned in the direction of the noise.

Probably an animal. A raccoon, perhaps, or a fox.

But Thomas knew that it sounded somehow different.

~~~

He made the long trek back to the lodge and found his parents sitting in the chairs at the lake's edge. Thomas leaned down to kiss his mother.

"How was your adventure?" asked Cindy.

"Awesome," answered Thomas. "It's a beautiful day. There was a bald eagle over the lake."

"We had a pretty eventful morning ourselves," said Chris Tucker. "An animal got into the cabin and ate the leftovers from breakfast off the stovetop before we had cleaned up. Let's all remember to make sure the door is closed completely."

Rain moved in over the lake and the woods that evening for hours. The Tuckers gathered and watched through the large window as rags of fog moved in over the lake. Chris lit a fire in the hearth and opened a board game. Cindy made popcorn in a pan with a lid on top and held it over the flames. Like firecrackers in a Lunar New Year parade, the kernels began to pop with increasing intensity.

Outside, over the constant pattering of the rain, out near the woods, eruptions of laughter could be heard emanating from the small wooden cabin.

~~~

Early the next morning, Chris and Thomas took an old metal canoe out onto the lake. Father and son paddled, oars dipping into the crystalline water. They ventured farther and farther across Lake Wanagi. The lake stretched over forty miles, with bays and tributaries and creeks to explore, as well as islands and inlets. There were over 1,200 miles of shoreline, with nearly as many Native American legends and myths surrounding it all.

"You and mom okay?" Thomas asked from the back of the canoe. They had crossed a good section of the lake, getting closer to the other side.

"Yeah, why?" Chris answered his son.

"I don't know. You guys seem a little down. Especially mom. You know, dad, just because I'm getting older, doesn't mean I won't continue to come up here. One day I will probably bring your grandkids with me."

Chris stopped rowing and the canoe skimmed across the placid surface.

"I'm sorry, Thomas. We don't mean to cast a funk over the trip. It's not the vacation," said Chris Tucker, oar on his lap. "It's the fact that we're getting older. You're getting older. We're proud of you. We just miss our little boy."

"I know," said Thomas. "I'm sorry, dad."

"I think you leaving the house has made mom think about Emma, too. She'd be thirteen. We came up here just after she was born."

Thomas looked down.

Chris turned around to face his son. "We raised a great son. We're very lucky."

Thomas didn't say anything. He stared off, beyond his dad, to the shoreline on the other side of the lake.

"What?" Chris Tucker said, turning back, towards the front of the canoe.

There, fifty yards out, across the water on a short-wooded bluff, was a little girl, maybe seven or eight with matted brown hair. She had a hand raised to her mouth, as if pondering the appearance of the men in the silver craft.

"What on earth?" said Chris Tucker.

Thomas started paddling in the girl's direction. His father raised a hand, motioning for his son to stop.

"Easy," said Chris Tucker. "We don't want to scare her."

"But, dad, she may need our help!"

"No … no. I don't think so. Go slowly."

The girl lowered her head and squinted her dark-shadowed eyes their direction. A hawk circled overhead, crying out. The canoe drew closer. Forty yards. Thirty. The girl wore a dirty blue jumper with a light blue T-shirt underneath. She was barefoot.

The canoe edged closer. And, then, in an instant, like a frightened animal, she was gone into the forest.

Father and son paddled with determination. But there was no easy place to land the canoe. The shoreline where the girl had been, just moments before, rose from the cold water, a stubby wall of iron ore five feet straight up. Chris and Thomas paddled on, finally locating an area where the land gently met the lake. Chris jumped out into the shallow cold water. He pulled the canoe to shore.

"That little girl was too young to be out here alone," he said.

"What is she doing out here?" asked Thomas.

"I don't know. There are no campgrounds or lodges on this part of the lake. We have to make sure she's okay."

"But she ran away."

"She's scared, now come on."

They dragged the canoe in and headed up the shoreline, navigating over rocks, through tall brush, and around trees. They made their way to the very spot where the little girl had been standing only moments earlier. Chris examined the surrounding brush. There was a faint path leading away from the lake, into the forest.

They followed it. In places where the sun was blocked by the trees, the trail grew damp and muddy. Thomas spotted something and crouched down.

"Look," he said to his father.

A child's footprint.

They continued on, deeper and deeper into the forest. A chorus of birds chirped.

"Hello!" Chris yelled, his voice trailing off into the woodland.

A white-tailed deer shot out from behind an aspen tree, surprising them, as it bounded off into the deeps of the forest.

"Don't be afraid!" called Chris. "We want to help you!"

But the forest was still. Chris and Thomas walked on. Searching. Soon the muddy path through the woods disappeared.

"We can't give up." Chris said. "That little girl doesn't belong out here. Not alone."

They walked down a slope to a clear flowing creek. Chris was the first to spot it, across the water, a large piece of old plywood with two tall sticks holding one end up—a lean-to. Underneath the shelter were several old rusted tin cans. But there was one that wasn't weathered. It was new and still had the paper label on it. It was a can of organic chickpeas. The label was from a high-end grocery store—the same market that the Tucker family shopped at back home.

"Something is not right here," said Chris to his son.

"That's ours," said Thomas. "We brought that up here. I bet it was taken yesterday when you said an animal got into the cabin."

"I don't get this, Thomas. Is there some little girl who lives in the woods out here? It's impossible. This doesn't make any sense at all."

Chris Tucker stood and looked around. And then he had a crazy thought. Could it be? Could it be her? As impossible, implausible, and out of the question and the realm of reality as it all seemed, Chris Tucker had a feeling in the pit of his very stomach, even in his heart, a sorrow he had only felt once before. At that moment, he believed in the impossible.

He reached into his pocket and pulled out a pewter compass with a glass dial. He looked at it for a moment and then bent down beneath the lean-to and set the compass on the earthen floor.

"You're leaving that?" his son asked. "But that was grandpa's. He gave that to you when you were a kid."

"It's okay," said Chris Tucker. "I don't need it anymore."

He smiled. "I was eleven when he gave it to me. He said it was to help me find my way."

"Why are you leaving it?"

"To help her find her way. Now, come on. Let's head back. We've looked long enough. I don't think we're going to find her."

"Shouldn't we report this to the police or to the forestry service?"

"Yes. But first I want to talk to Mr. Dunn. He may be able to shed some light on this. He's lived here longer than just about anyone."

Chris and Thomas turned, leaving behind the small round pewter compass sitting on the ground underneath the lean-to.

It was midday when they returned. Cindy was gone, out for a hike. The shades were drawn on the main residence of the resort, a three-bedroom house where Mr. Dunn lived. The camp owner always took an afternoon nap.

That evening, Mr. Dunn set the wood for a fire. Cindy had returned, everyone cleaned up after the hearty supper, and the family walked down to the lakeshore.

"Chris," Cindy said, "please, you have to call the police about this. That poor, poor baby. She's out there. She needs our help."

"I will," said Chris Tucker. "I just want to see what Mr. Dunn knows. Perhaps there's a rational explanation. Maybe there's a residence in the forest where a family lives. Maybe there's a lodge we don't know about on that side of the lake."

Yet even as Chris Tucker said these words, he was becoming more convinced of another answer.

"Good evening, Tucker family!" called Mr. Dunn, seeing them approach. "And how was our day of expeditions and adventures?"

Chris smiled. They all settled into the old weathered Adirondack chairs.

"Mr. Dunn," said Chris Tucker. "We had a little surprise today."

"Did you?"

"Indeed. Thomas and I were canoeing on the other side of the lake, near Spaulding Bay. We saw a little girl, standing on the shoreline. When we approached, she ran off faster than a jackrabbit."

A look fell across Mr. Dunn's face. He sat down in his chair, staring across the dark lake. "Well I'll be ..."

"What is it, Mr. Dunn?" asked Cindy.

"It's been so long," he said. "I thought, well, I thought perhaps she was gone. Maybe she had found some peace, at last."

"Who?" Chris asked with urgency.

"Francine, of course. Francine McClure."

The Tuckers were incredulous. The fire popped.

"You mean the little girl who was lost in the woods back in the '50s?" asked Cindy.

"Yes," said Mr. Dunn, still staring across the lake.

"Mr. Dunn," said Cindy. "That's not possible."

"I'm afraid it is, Cindy. It is all too possible."

Chris Tucker ran his hands on the armrests of the chair.

"After she went missing, a few people claimed to have seen her, wandering, out there." Mr. Dunn nodded to the dark lake and the wilds beyond. "As if she was still looking for her family. A restless spirit. There are many Native American myths just like that, you know. A spirit that cannot find peace until it finds answers. She just wanted to find her mother and father."

"Then, over the years, there were fewer sightings—fewer and fewer reports of a little girl with brown hair and eyes and a blue dress. But every so often—every few years—someone would go to the authorities, some camper or a hiker or person in a canoe just like yourselves, and they'd report seeing her, a little girl lost forever, living somewhere out there, in the shadows behind the trees."

A fish jumped from the surface of the lake, making a splash.

"Then the sightings dwindled down to a scant few, just once every generation or so. Usually it was another child who saw her. Francine. Poor Francine. I thought, perhaps, she had finally given up. She had finally gone. I guess I was wrong."

"But Mr. Dunn, you don't believe all that, do you?' asked Cindy Tucker.

"Yes," said Chris Tucker. "Yes, he does."

"That's right, I do."

"Have you ever seen her?" asked Thomas.

Mr. Dunn was quiet for a moment, mournful. "Only once," he answered, at last. "Only once. Many years back."

"Well, how can we bring her peace?" asked Thomas, "if what you say is true."

"I don't believe there is a way to bring her peace," said Mr. Dunn. "She is looking for her family."

The fire danced. A few bands of thin clouds moved in over the lake, partially obstructing the light from the half moon.

"So we're not going to report this to the police?" Cindy said. "With all due respect, I don't believe in ghosts. I think you saw a real little girl out there today who needs our help."

"Darling," said Chris Tucker. "I'll go to town first thing in the morning. I'll report the sighting. But didn't you hear what Mr. Dunn said? Sightings have been going on for years—decades even. I had a feeling when I saw her, a feeling I've never experienced before. It was like a strange paternal instinct. Like when in the middle of the night, when Thomas was just a baby sleeping in another room, and he woke. He didn't have to make a noise. Not a sound. But a parent knows. They know their baby is up. I had that feeling. A part of me knew who that girl was right away. I knew."

218

Cindy sighed. "This is crazy."

She stood. "I love all of you. I'm going to read and go to bed." She walked back to the cabin.

"We just have to leave her be," said Mr. Dunn, turning to Chris Tucker. "I so wish there was something we could do. Believe me, I've thought about it all over the years. I've agonized over it. How to help that poor wandering spirit."

Chris and Thomas and Mr. Dunn sat in silence.

~~~

The next morning, before the sun catapulted over the lake, Chris Tucker woke and dressed in his boots and blue jeans, a warm flannel shirt. It was a crisp morning, a loon somewhere in the woods called out.

Chris closed the front door behind him and looked down at his feet. There, on the stoop, was his pewter compass. He picked it up.

"I'll be damned," he said, softly, turning the compass in his palm.

He looked out at the dark woods around him, slipping the compass in his pocket.

~~~

The nearest town of any size, Grand Falls, was just over an hour away. Daybreak arrived. Upon his arrival, Chris found a diner, had a hot cup of coffee and some oatmeal. He read the local newspaper and waited until 8:30 am, when the local library opened.

The old Carnegie Library was a large limestone turn-of-the century building partially covered in ivy. Chris Tucker approached it just as a young woman, in blue-framed glasses and a T-shirt with an art deco rocket, unlocked the double front oak doors.

"Good morning," she said as Chris Tucker approached. "Can I help you?"

"Good morning. I was hoping you could help me find something," he said.

"That's what I'm here for. I'm one of the librarians," she said.

Inside the entranceway, with its high ceilings and marble floor, Chris felt it was more temple than athenaeum.

"I'm looking for some information on a little girl who went missing in the '50s out at Lake Wanagi," Chris said.

"You mean Francine McClure," she said.

"You know of her?"

"That story is sort of a folktale in these parts. Come with me, we have a room for local and regional history. There's an entire file on her."

Chris followed her into a room near the back of the building. It was small, with two large wooden tables with green banker's lamps atop them. Rows of filing cabinets lined the back wall. The librarian opened a drawer and withdrew a folder bulging with newspaper clippings and papers.

"Here it is," she said, handing the material over to Chris. "Let me know if you need anything else. I'll be at the reference desk."

Chris thanked her, and she left the room. He sat down at one of the old library tables. The loose papers were not organized in any particular fashion. On top was a twenty-five-year-old item from the local newspaper:

Hikers Claim to See Ghost of Missing Girl

Chris scanned the short article about a husband and wife who reported seeing the figure of a little girl standing on a tree-lined ridge in the forest by Lake Wanagi. When they approached her, the girl ran off. Local authorities investigated the sighting but found no trace of the girl. The article went on to quote a local police spokesman, saying the description of the girl was similar to purported sightings over the years, of Francine McClure, an eight-year-old who went missing in the forest in 1953.

Chris continued to flip through the papers and found more of the same.

The most recent sighting, however, was the one he had found on top, a quarter-century old. As he went through the file, he discovered more and more frequent sightings of the little girl in the sixties and seventies, going all the way back to the time she went missing. The stories were all the same. The same little girl. Brown hair. Brown eyes. Blue overall dress with light blue short-sleeved shirt underneath. They would spot her and she would run away. Page after page, paper after paper, always the same. Francine McClure would appear, somewhere in the woods or on the lakeshore or on some far-off hill, only to vanish as quickly as she had arrived.

He kept flipping through the articles. Then, he found a front-page headline, dated October 20, 1967. There was a photograph. Two men riding horses in the woods saw a little girl standing off in the distance, on the far side of a creek. They snapped a single picture before she ran away. The photo was slightly out of focus, an old Kodachrome snapshot, four-by-four with vanilla borders. The image was unmistakable. Chris drew the clipping closer to his face. There she was. The brown hair. The dark eyes. The little jumper. The bare feet. Looking right at the camera.

Francine McClure.

"Good God," Chris said quietly.

He turned to the next article in the file folder, another front-page story, this one dated October 19, 1953.

Girl, 8, Missing

It was the first news story. The first report. Francine McClure, age 8, of Sterling Springs, Illinois, vacationing with her parents. Lost.

Chris read on. And then, stopped. He couldn't believe his eyes. The story went on to interview William Dunn, proprietor of the Edgerton Resort, where the girl had been vacationing. The parents went out in a canoe and the young

William Dunn had agreed to watch their daughter. He turned his back for no more than a minute and she was gone. Lost in the wilderness.

Search parties were called in. Volunteers from the area helped look for her. After several weeks, the weather turned and all hope was lost. The search and rescue became a search and recovery, and, then, with the arrival of winter, people had mostly given up altogether.

Chris Tucker leaned back in his chair and exhaled. The librarian walked into the room.

"Did you find what you were looking for?" she asked.

"Oh, yes." Chris said.

"It's quite a story. Sad."

"Yes, it is."

Chris closed the folder, thanked the librarian, and headed back towards Lake Wanagi, back to the Edgerton Resort. There was no need to report his sighting to the authorities.

~~~

It was afternoon when he arrived. Thomas had taken a small motorboat out to fish. Cindy was knitting in the living room and looking out on the lake.

"How was your trip to Grand Falls? What did the police say?"

"I didn't go to the police, Cindy," said Chris. "We didn't see a little girl. We saw a lost soul looking for her family."

Cindy looked long at her husband. "Chris. That's impossible."

"No, no it's not."

Cindy shook her head. "This trip has been difficult, Chris. With Thomas leaving the house. It's made me think. About Emma. About giving birth to her and that feeling of elation. Only to have her cold body rest on my chest until the doctors took her away as I sobbed. I just wanted to hold her one last time.

I knew I would never touch that perfect skin again. I would never see those perfect eyes that never opened. We came up here right after that. That was our first trip. You're thinking about Emma, too. You're replacing her with some wild notion of a little ghost girl who needs your love. Chris, ghosts aren't real. They don't exist. This is just your sorrow."

~~~

That evening, after Thomas had returned from fishing, after Mr. Dunn had woken from his afternoon nap, after supper, they all gathered at the lake, by the fire.

"You went to town, I hear?" said Mr. Dunn.

"I did," said Chris.

"And did you report your sighting of little Francine to the police?"

"I didn't need to. You were right."

"So, what did you do?"

"I went to the library. I read up on the story of Francine McClure."

Mr. Dunn shifted in his chair. Cindy and Thomas were quiet.

"Then you know what happened," he said.

"Why didn't you tell us, Mr. Dunn? Why didn't you tell us that you were the owner of the Edgerton back then? That you were watching her when she was lost?"

William Dunn sat still. He looked at the family. He looked out to the lake. He looked to the ground.

"Shame, I guess. Remorse. Denial. A mixture of all of those and much more."

Fog rolled in off the lake, up the shoreline, drifting towards the edge of the forest behind them.

"It was a mistake, Mr. Dunn. A terrible, sad tragic mistake, but a mistake nonetheless."

"Oh, it's much more than that, Chris," said Mr. Dunn. "So much more. She was on my watch. Under my wing, and I lost her. A little bird out of the nest. I will never forgive myself. Never."

Mr. Dunn's eyes grew teary.

"We looked for weeks. Scoured the forest. Brought in horses and dogs. When the first frost came and folks had given up hope, I continued to look. Francine. Oh, Francine. Every day I went out there, to the woods, and I called out her name. Francine.

"Then, one late afternoon, after the first baby's breath of snow had fallen and the sun set upon it all pink, I saw her, just like you did yesterday. She was standing far off amongst the trees, looking at me. I was overjoyed. Elated. The good Lord had answered all my prayers. At last, I had found her! And then, the darnedest thing happened. I couldn't believe it. She ran away. Gone. Forever. Why? It was then that I knew the truth. She lives now in these woods, with me, to haunt me for my terrible, terrible mistake."

"Mr. Dunn," said Cindy, "You can't think that. You must forgive yourself."

"How could I? Those poor parents had to leave and drive hundreds of miles and go home without their baby. Could you imagine that? Leaving without your child? And I was to blame. That's why I never married. Why I never had children. I couldn't bear the responsibility. I heard that the father passed sometime in the late Seventies. He never had closure. And the mother, she has lived long, sad days. Oh, we wrote a few times. I tried to stay in touch, but for what? To remind her of the day her life was destroyed? A dear woman, she was. Susan McClure. As far as I know she may still be alive and as old and as sad as I am."

The fog was thicker now, rolling in off the surface of the lake. No one knew what to say.

"And so, dear Tuckers, that is the tragic story of Francine McClure. It is her spirit that wanders these woods. There is a reason that most of the sightings of her have been by children and families. She is curious. She just wants to know the love that she lost."

Chris Tucker stood and put a hand on the old man's shoulder. "Mr. Dunn. We love you. You may think you never had a family, but you have been a family to us. All these years. You understand that? We love you."

Chris Tucker turned and walked back to the cabin. And there at the edge of the woods, standing in the mist, he saw her, looking right at him. Her face was muddied, her hair tangled. She was barefoot, wearing the blue overall dress and the light blue T-shirt. She made a step from the forest, out into the clearing. Chris stopped in his tracks. She made another step forward.

He stood still, his heart leaping. Slowly she walked out, towards him. The family far down at the lake sat in quietude, their backs to the encounter. Chris Tucker stood motionless as little Francine, unsure, edged closer.

She walked up to him. Looking up and reaching out with her small hand. There was mud under her chipped fingernails.

Chris Tucker slowly extended his hand and they touched. They held hands for a moment—the father looking down at the little girl. For a second, Chris had a strange feeling that Francine actually wanted him to take her home. To load her in the car so she could, at long last, have a family again. But that would be impossible. He knew it, and, looking into those dark eyes, she knew it, too.

Chris Tucker smiled at Francine.

She wants to feel the love she barely knew.

He squeezed her little hand and stroked the top of her head.

And then, Francine let go of Chris Tucker and turned and walked back toward the edge of the woods. She looked, one last time at him, before gliding into the fog and the shadows behind the trees.

End of Summer

Beyond the fringe of suburbia, beyond the circuit board of cul-de-sacs and pre-fab homes, out past the strip of soulless big box stores and interchangeable auto dealerships, far past the last country cemetery on the outskirts of town where Mrs. O'Brien is buried, far out into the fields of moonscape dirt and lion-hued stubble, we walked.

Me and the Stickman and Mib.

It was September and the last day of summer. The sunlight was white and had let go of its August bakery-oven warmth. When you are young, fifteen, and you live where the suburbs vanish and the rural begins, you walk a lot. You explore.

Stickman was a year younger than me. He was skeleton tall and skeleton thin.

Mib was my thirteen-year-old mutt of many mysterious breeds, black and white and spotted and long-haired and runty. And sweet.

The days were shorter, darker, sadder. Weekends like this were miniscule islands, rocks in the creek of the institutional school week to step upon.

The sky was monochromatic, a hardware paint-sample strip of various grays. In the wind there was cinder and ash; golden-rod and thistle; fallen leaf and pumpkin and honeycrisp apple. Hell, maybe it carried with it witch cauldron double, double toil and trouble, candy corn, cinnamon stick, dust of monarch migration, dandelion puff, homecoming bonfire, early love, Indian summer.

Well, maybe that wasn't in the air, but it sure seems like it was.

We walked. Mib out exploring in front of us. No leash. Free. Sniffing every prairie dog hole and cow patty.

Red barns in the distance. A lone Cessna far up in the sky, navigating the winds. We walked out in the fields with the huge electrical towers in the distance, steel lattice and humming high voltage spider-line draping on to the end of the earth.

Mib panted. When he was happy, content, he had a smile. Pink tongue and tartar teeth. Me and Stick talked about school and our favorite bands and our favorite movies. And we missed Danny. He used to walk with us, too.

"It's weird without him," Stickman said as we moved along. We were the only ones in the world in that place at that moment. "It's like an empty space in a missing man plane formation."

Danny loved military jets. He would have understood what Stick had said.

But with a Houdini snap of a finger, Danny was gone. We could make no sense of it.

Thank God I still had the Stickman. My friend. Walking with me, here and there. Down the road, we wouldn't always stay in touch. We would move on.

I closed my eyes and we walked.

Live Forever!

He took a deep breath, dusted his lapels, adjusted his tie, and rang the doorbell. William Joy was standing on the front steps of Ray Bradbury's house. Ray Bradbury, famous author of *Fahrenheit 451*, *The Martian Chronicles*, *Something Wicked This Way Comes*. Some people have said William looked like a young Ray Bradbury, with his crew cut and black horn-rimmed glasses.

The house was painted a sunny dandelion yellow and was tucked into a sloping green parcel in the old Los Angeles neighborhood of Cheviot Hills. Eucalyptus and palm trees and leafy shrubs rustled in the warm California breeze, creating a rush of sound that resonated like a conch shell held to the ear. William looked down at his feet. The doormat had three ghosts printed on it with the word "BOO!" above them.

The front door slowly creaked open and an attractive, well-dressed woman with a 1940s-style hairdo answered.

"May I help you?"

William was startled for a moment, for the woman looked remarkably similar to pictures he had seen of Ray Bradbury's late wife Maggie, when she was a young woman. William looked down and saw that the woman was holding a feather duster and concluded she was most likely the housekeeper.

"Hello," William said, clearing his throat. "I'm here for a one o'clock interview with Mr. Bradbury."

He could hardly believe he had just said those words. William had worshipped Ray Bradbury for so long. Ray Bradbury was the reason he became a writer. And here he was, a staff reporter for the *St. Louis Post-Journal*, writing a story on the renowned, Midwestern-born author. At thirty-three-years-old, William had written hundreds of stories, interviewed movie stars, rock stars, musicians, artists, politicians. But this, he had to admit, this was a dream come true.

"Won't you come in?" the housekeeper said, smiling and beckoning with her hand. "He is expecting you."

William stepped into the foyer. Hanging on the wall was a large painting of the famous Bradbury character, "The Illustrated Man." It was an original from an old book cover. William knew it well. He had carried the paperback with that very cover on it when he was teenager: It was frayed from being toted around during the day in the back pocket of well-worn blue jeans and read under the warmth of bed covers long after midnight.

"Good afternoon!" a voice bellowed, breaking William's trance. He knew that voice! He wheeled around and looked down three steps. Standing in the spacious living room was the man known as "the world's greatest living science-fiction writer": Ray Douglas Bradbury. He was dressed in snow-white tennis shoes, white socks pulled high up his calves, white tennis shorts, and a crisp, freshly starched blue oxford underneath a white windbreaker. He was wearing a tie emblazoned with colorful Easter eggs loosely around his neck.

"Come in, come in!" he said, motioning William into the living room. The young writer stepped forward and shook Bradbury's thick, surprisingly strong hand.

"Hello, Mr. Bradbury. I can't tell you what a great honor this is. I'm sure you hear it all the time, but I grew up reading your books." William was speaking rather quickly, even to his own ears.

"Tell me more, tell me more! I like you already!" Ray Bradbury said, smiling.

William sat down on a small floral print sofa. He nervously dug out his pad, pen, and recorder from his bag. He wanted to compose himself, think of something clever to say. Two cats darted about the room, moving swiftly underneath end tables and behind furniture. Sunlight poured in through the open white plantation shutters.

"'The time traveler, after one hundred years of silence, had agreed to be interviewed. He was, on this day one-hundred-and-thirty years old. And this afternoon, at four o'clock sharp, Pacific time, was the anniversary of his one and only journey in time,'" quoted William.

"You're amazing!" Ray Bradbury said, beaming. "'The Toynbee Convector!' It's one of my personal favorites."

"I've read all of your work, Mr. Bradbury," said William. "All your novels, plays, screenplays, poetry, essays, and the more than six hundred short stories. As you can see, I am a great admirer and you have had a *profound* influence on me."

"Thank you."

"I'm curious, who are some of the people who influenced you?" William asked.

Ray Bradbury crossed the living room. At eighty-six, he moved with energy and much grace. He went to a bookcase and picked up a framed picture and handed it to William. It was an original animation cel from the Walt Disney film, *Snow White*.

"I met Walt Disney by sheer happenstance," said Ray Bradbury, "a random encounter in a Beverly Hills Department store. It was Christmas, 1964."

From that point forward, until Disney's death just two years later, Ray Bradbury said they forged a fast friendship based on their mutual love of world's fairs and cartoons and architecture and the mysterious and glorious nature of creativity itself. As William Joy listened to Ray Bradbury recount the friendship, he marveled at this singular relationship. Disney and Bradbury. Two idea men. Two visionaries.

The sun outside lowered toward the horizon, sinking out there, somewhere over the shimmering Pacific three miles from the Bradbury home. The housekeeper entered the living room, offering them a glass of red wine. She turned on the old green bankers lamps as dusk settled outside. William looked at Ray Bradbury, sitting in a chair, sipping his wine. He began recounting his ill-fated relationship with film director John Huston. He spent six trying months in late 1953 and early 1954 holed up in a Dublin, Ireland, hotel writing the screenplay for the Huston adaptation of the Melville classic, *Moby-Dick*. As late autumn rain turned into early winter snow falling all across Ireland, it was a trying time for Bradbury: Huston was a complex, difficult man and the Melville tome was a difficult, complex book to adapt. But he did it. He finished the screenplay and was darned proud of the end product.

"Work is the only answer," said Ray Bradbury. "If you're having a bad day, even if you accomplish just a little bit, you feel better about yourself."

Bradbury still wrote every day. He was full of philosophies and ideas and an abiding hunger to create. As Bradbury spoke of his working relationships with Huston and Disney, he brought up other friends and William just watched and thought that this man was a walking encyclopedia of 20th century popular culture. He was a time machine. He had been close with the great Italian filmmaker Federico Fellini. He had worked for Alfred Hitchcock. Once, in 1992, he had even been the special guest at a dinner with the former president of the Soviet Union, Mikhail Gorbachev.

Ray Bradbury had lived an incredible life and, as William sat there in the living room, twirling his wine in his glass and staring at it as it went round and round, he was already struggling in his mind at the complexity of the feature story he would write. Bradbury had truly lived the life fantastic. How would William get it all into a three-thousand-word feature for his newspaper?

"You mustn't overthink when you write," Bradbury said, perceiving William's anxiety. "The faster you blurt, the more swiftly you write, the more honest you are. I always tell writers that a first draft must come quickly and only with the rewrites can you begin intellectualizing your work."

Bradbury took a sip of his wine and then chortled.

"More succinctly, just throw up in the morning and clean it up in the afternoon!"

They both laughed. They had hit it off so well. Part of the connection was that they were both Midwesterners: They had explored prairie creeks and ravines and fields when they were boys (albeit separated by nearly a half century). When they talked architecture, they found they had the same favorites: "The Chrysler Building is the greatest building of the 20th century!" Bradbury declared. They talked about painters, film directors, writers, restaurants, jazz artists, science, religion, and politics. But most of all, they talked Bradbury. As nighttime fully settled outside, William still couldn't quite believe he was sitting with this great icon of Americana.

It didn't seem real.

Bradbury didn't seem real. He seemed more a character out of history. Truly. When this man was a little boy he watched Civil War veterans march in parades down the main street of his boyhood town. When he grew up and became synonymous with science fiction, he traveled to the Johnson Space Center in Houston, Texas, to interview the Apollo astronauts for *Life* magazine. From the veterans of Sherman's march to the sea to the veterans of the Sea of Tranquility, Ray Bradbury had witnessed a miraculous period in world history—undoubtedly the greatest period of technological advancement in the history of humankind.

"Why have you written so often about space travel?" William asked.

"Space is the only answer. If we stay on this little blue planet, we're all doomed. The sun will eventually burn out. But going out into space will ensure that the human race will live forever."

The interview continued. They finished the bottle of wine.

"Can you return tomorrow?" Ray Bradbury asked. "I'm enjoying this and there's much I haven't told you."

William was dumbfounded. Bradbury actually wanted him to come back for further interviews. "Of course, Mr. Bradbury, I would be honored."

~~~

William returned to the sprawling dandelion yellow house as instructed the next morning, and climbed the stairs and rang the bell and was ushered in by the maid.

"He'll be right with you," she said, leaving William alone in the living room.

William looked at the hundreds of books that lined the built-in shelves. He looked at all the awards and medals and various trophies Ray Bradbury had amassed over the decades. Then he spotted a small-framed black and white photograph and picked it up. It was a weathered picture of a young Ray Bradbury and Marguerite McClure, taken during their courtship. William knew this as Ray Bradbury had written "1946" at the top of the photograph. It was one year before their marriage. In the picture, the couple were cheek to cheek, obviously in the throes of love. William stared at it for a long while, looking closer and closer at the future Maggie Bradbury. Brunette hair. A round, supple face the shade of soft moonlight. Full lips adorned by a deep shade of lipstick.

It was uncanny. William couldn't get over it. Then he heard someone behind him and turned around. The maid was standing there, looking at William.

"I look like her, don't I?" she asked.

"It's remarkable," William replied. And it was. The maid was an identical match to the woman in the old photograph.

And then, reliable as an old Timex, Ray Bradbury rounded a corner and stepped down into the living room.

"Good morning!" he exclaimed, as the maid wandered off to another room in the house.

Again, the two men spent the better part of the day sitting and talking. Bradbury told of his fateful encounter with an enigmatic carnival worker named "Mr. Electrico."

It was Labor Day Weekend, 1932. A dingy and dusty carnival had arrived and pitched tents along the rocky shoreline of Lake Michigan in Ray Bradbury's boyhood town of Waukegan, Illinois. It was a gray, gauzy day. A light rain was falling.

Twelve-year-old bespectacled, tow-headed Ray was in love with carnivals and circuses and sideshow freaks. On that day, he wandered into a tattered magician's tent and took a seat alongside a dozen other children on a sawdust covered floor. The lights dimmed. Mr. Electrico emerged from behind a curtain wearing a black cape. He was wielding a heavy Excalibur sword. The mysterious magician with his great shock of white hair took a seat in an electric chair and an assistant strapped him in. Then at a nod, the assistant pulled a lever from stage-left sending fifty thousand volts of pure, unfettered electricity coursing through the magician. Mr. Electrico's teeth chattered. His eyes glowed. His hair stood on end. Then the assistant pushed the lever back in place and the thunder and lightning show ended as quickly as it began. The assistant unstrapped the magician and Mr. Electrico picked up his sword and slowly walked up to all the children sitting before him. One by one he began tapping his sword on their brows as their hair stood up on end, electricity charging from magician through the sword and into the kids. The members in the audience were incredulous.

Then, finally, Mr. Electrico approached one last child, Ray Bradbury. He tapped the sword on the boy's left shoulder, then his right, then gently touched the tip of the sword to young Ray Bradbury's nose. The twelve-year-old could feel electricity triggering through every cell in his body and the magician and child locked eyes.

"LIVE FOREVER!" Mr. Electrico cried.

William sat and watched and listened and took close notes as the elderly writer excitedly conjured his younger self. William found the carnival tale both mesmerizing and metaphoric.

"Why did he say that to me?! Why?! He didn't say that to any of the other children!"

Two weeks after the incident, Ray Bradbury began writing short stories and he never stopped.

Predominant throughout the writing of Ray Bradbury was the theme of life and death, mortality and immortality, and the quest to live forever. And Ray Bradbury looked at art and creativity and writing as the one way to achieve this.

Before they knew it, the day was winding down and darkness was closing in over Los Angeles once again.

"This has been an amazing conversation! Come back every week!" Bradbury said.

"I wish I could," William said.

"Well," Bradbury said, finally, "we've talked and talked. I still haven't shown you my basement office. Do you want to take a quick look around?"

Ray Bradbury's basement office was storied. Fans across the globe knew about it from photos in magazines. It was the stuff of legend. It was a laboratory of the imagination. From photos William had seen of it over the years, and from television interviews taped there, the basement office was a wonderland of metaphors from Ray Bradbury's life. To the casual observer, it may have been mistaken for a junkyard, but to a Bradbury fan, it was a museum of magic and imagination.

By the kitchen, Ray Bradbury opened the door and ushered William down the short flight of stairs. The office was packed to the rafters—floor to ceiling—with trinkets and mementos from Bradbury's life. There were hundreds of copies of his own books lining shelves, rare editions, foreign editions, and first editions. There was his first collection, *Dark Carnival*, published in the spring of 1947. The basement office was also a veritable toy store. Old tin rocket shops and wind-up robots waited to spring to mechanized life. Rubber dinosaurs lined shelves. There were action figures and stuffed animals and hundreds of homemade gifts from fans over the decades: A painting of the Martian landscape here, a sculpture of a famous movie monster there, a handmade circus poster for Cooger & Dark's Pandemonium Shadow Show there.

William Joy was in heaven.

There were old, framed black-and-white photos of Ray Bradbury as a boy. Hanging on a wooden rafter above the desk was Ray's father's old dusty Stetson, a hat that had traveled across Depression-era America more than once. William spotted old autographs from Golden-era Hollywood screen legends, comic books and piles and piles of manila folders stacked high, each containing letters or press clippings. It was an amazing amusement park for a Bradbury die-hard.

The desk itself was piled high with old papers and letters and an IBM Selectric typewriter. The man who brought great fictional explorers out into the deeps of space did not own a computer.

In a corner of the office was a row of metal filing cabinets. William walked toward them and looked at the labels fixed in the middle of each drawer.

"NOVELS IN PROGRESS."

"SHORT STORIES IN PROGRESS."

"SCREENPLAYS IN PROGRESS."

William grew excited. How much unreleased Bradbury was there?

He turned and looked at Ray Bradbury, who was staring at him.

"You like this place," he declared.

"It's incredible!"

Bradbury looked down at the floor and was silent for a moment and said, "I've never told anyone this, not even my beloved wife of fifty-six years, God bless her soul. But I'd like to show you something. You must keep it a secret."

"Of course," William said. What was he alluding to?

"These last two days you have been here have been magical," he said. "I have enjoyed our talks."

"So have I."

"I feel a connection to you, and that is why I would like you to meet some of my friends. Would you like to meet them?"

"Of course." Now William's curiosity was piqued.

"Good. Then follow me."

Ray Bradbury walked slowly over to another door and opened it. It led down to a sub-basement, a level below them.

"Come with me."

Ray Bradbury began to descend the stairs and William followed. At the bottom of the steps Bradbury turned on a light and everything lit up.

William couldn't believe his eyes. Along with more books and more toys and more piles of papers and manuscripts and photos was something he just couldn't fathom. He closed his eyes and opened them again. It couldn't be. But it was.

Sitting in chairs were Walt Disney, George Burns, Alfred Hitchcock, an elderly, aristocratic man—most likely Renaissance scholar Bernard Berenson ... And in a corner, slumped in a chair, sound asleep, was film director John Huston himself.

"Oh ... my ... God," William said. "Are they ..."

"All my friends. My mentors," said Ray. "Living and in the flesh."

"You mean ... they're real?"

"Welcome!" said Walter Elias Disney, standing up and moving across the room to greet William. He was in his early sixties, the Uncle Walt America knew and loved. He was dressed in a finely tailored vintage wool suit, with a pencil thin tie.

"Good evening," said Hitchcock.

"How ya doin', kid?" said a youthful George Burns, puffing on a cigar. He was probably forty.

They rose and moved across the small room to shake William's hand. All of them, that is, except Huston, who remained in his chair, leaning gently to one side, eyes closed, his chin resting on his chest.

All the men were the exact age they had been when Ray Bradbury had worked with them.

Bradbury looked at William with excitement, his eyes electric.

"What's with John Huston?" he said, motioning to the sleeping director.

"Don't mind him, kid," said Burns. "We turned him off, he was annoying us."

"Turned him off?" William asked.

And then he understood. Walt Disney was standing closest to him, smelling of a gentle, expensive, cologne. William heard something faint, something odd. A whirring of motors, a spinning of metal cogs and wheels. There was an almost imperceptible mechanized symphony inside of Walt Disney.

Of course! Animatrons.

William had seen them many times before at Disneyland and Disneyworld and Epcot Center. The Mechanized Abraham Lincoln and the robotic Pirates of the Caribbean.

"They're astounding!" he said, looking at Ray Bradbury who was beaming with pride.

"They were built from the ground up by my genius friends at Disney Imagineering," he said like a proud papa. "Every cogwheel, every cam, every capstan. A gyroscope here, a gizmo there, all brought to glorious life by thousands of

241

volts of primordial electricity—a hundred summer heat-lighting storms captured inside each of them. They will outlive both of us. As long as they are maintained, they will live forever."

The animatrons stared at William. It was both amazing and unsettling. A little shiver went up William's spine. He poked gently into George Burns. He felt real enough.

"Watch who you're poking, kid," George Burns said, taking another puff on his cigar.

William stayed in the basement for a good two or three hours, talking to them all. Berenson dottered around the small basement speaking of the art of properly visiting a museum. Disney discussed his dreams for Epcot as a laboratory to experiment on global issues such as urban congestion, space exploration, and environmentalism. It was almost as good as talking to the real McCoys. But as the hour neared midnight, it was time for William to leave.

"It's getting late," said Ray Bradbury. "I have a busy day tomorrow."

The animatrons shook William's hand and said good night and then they returned to the chairs they had been sitting in when he had arrived. William climbed the stairs and Ray Bradbury followed, turning off the lights and closing the basement door behind them.

"Well," he said. "I suppose it's back to the Midwest for you tomorrow?"

"I have an amazing story to write. But of course," William added, "what you have just shown me will remain a secret."

Ray Bradbury ushered William to the front door. The venerable author was quiet for a moment and said, "You are my bastard son, you know that? We're joined at the hip, you and I."

"Oh, Mr. Bradbury, to hear you say that ... it's such an honor. I can't thank you enough. This has been a dream. An incredible experience."

Ray Bradbury opened the door and William looked out at the dark Los Angeles night. He could hear the sound of crickets and the faint rush of traffic from the Santa Monica freeway. He turned to hug Ray Bradbury and say good-bye. But as William put his arms around Ray Bradbury, he heard it. It couldn't be, yet it was. Good God. The faint symphony. The symphony of machinery. All the cogs and whirring of little motors inside of him.

Ray Bradbury was not real.

William stepped back, dazed and bewildered.

"What's wrong?" asked Bradbury.

"Nothing," said William, collecting himself. He took a deep breath. "Again, I can't thank you enough."

"No, thank you."

William walked down the steps in complete and total confusion.

~~~

William Joy went back to his hotel room near Los Angeles International Airport and spent the majority of the night tossing and turning, unable to sleep. He paced the room, staring blankly out the floor to ceiling windows at the starkly illuminated airport and all the incoming jumbo jets arriving with precision throughout the night.

By the time the black of night turned pre-dawn cobalt, William was still trying to get his mind wrapped around what had happened at the Bradbury house the day before. His return flight to St. Louis was scheduled for late morning. He packed his bag, dressed, and as the sun rose, he decided to drive his rental car over to Cheviot Hills for one last visit with Ray Bradbury—that is, with Ray Bradbury's robot. William had to know what it was all about.

He climbed the stairs for the third time in as many days and rang the bell and the maid answered with a smile and ushered him in.

Bradbury was sitting in the living room with a pen in his hand, writing on a pad of paper.

"How wonderful!" he bellowed, looking up. "You returned!"

The maid left, and William stepped into the living room and took a seat.

"Mr. Bradbury," William said, "the friends you introduced me to yesterday ... the animatrons."

"Yes," he said. "Aren't they incredible? I'm never lonely now!"

William paused, inhaled, struggled for words. "Sir, when you are standing near them, you can hear the motors inside them, you can hear all the mechanized parts moving."

"Yes, they are complex machines, made of a million and one minuscule components."

"Sir," said William nervously. "When I stand next to you, I ... I hear the same noise. I hear the million and one components whirring away."

Ray Bradbury stared at William through his thick, black-rimmed glasses. "What are you saying?" he said, at last.

"Sir, where is the *real* Ray Bradbury?"

Ray Bradbury was silent for a long, uncomfortable moment with a look of bewilderment on his face. He glanced blankly at the floor, listening ... listening ... listening.

"Well, I'll be damned," he said.

"What?" William asked.

"I hear it. The million and one components. All the cogs and the wheels. I guess I've never noticed it before. I thought that was just normal. And you're saying it's not?"

"No. No, it's not."

It took all of William's courage to ask, again, "Sir, where is the real Ray Bradbury? Did he build you? Is he still alive?"

The electric Bradbury was bewildered. Lost. Confused. Silent for a long moment and then his eyes glassed over and a tear started to run down the side of his nose and across his cheek. The old machine was still. Thoughtful. Processing.

"If what you say is true, that I am machine, perhaps built by your literary Gepetto, then who knows? Ray Bradbury could be anywhere. I just don't know."

The Ray Bradbury machine stood up and moved to the center of the living room.

"With the know-how to build a machine like this, your Ray Bradbury could do anything. He could build a time machine! He might hopscotch the space-time continuum, leap-frog from 19th Dynasty Ramesses Egypt to Jurassic jungle and back to Green Town, Illinois, 1928, and still make it for a Swedish meatball dinner prepared steaming hot and with loving care by none other than his mother, Esther Marie Moberg Bradbury. Afterward, he could transport to Antietam to sniff the first salvo of acrid gun-powder drifting off on sad Maryland winds. Here he is walking the rain-slicked Avenue de l'Opera during the jazz age, next he's off to far Schenectady, with a stop off in Dublin at Heeber Finn's Pub for a pint of Guinness with the boyos circa winter 1954! Or, perhaps, the answer is more obvious ... Perhaps he is on Mars."

William looked at the robot and instantly regretted coming back to the house this third time. He should have left things as they were. He should never have told the machine that he was, in fact, just a machine. Because he was more than that. He was fantastic. He crackled with enthusiasm and energy and life. Now the machine stood there with his eyes glazed with tears and a look of defeated confusion on his face.

"I'm sorry," William said. "I'm sorry."

"It's okay," Ray Bradbury said, at last. "Foolish me for not noticing it until now. I guess you ... live ... with something for so long you just don't notice it."

And then he laughed.

"Funny thing. I'm not alive at all, am I?"

"Yes, you are," William said. "More than anyone I know."

And with that, William turned and said goodbye again, for the last time. He walked to the front door and closed it behind himself and stood in the cool Los Angeles morning and closed his eyes and took a deep breath. And he listened. And then he heard it. Inside himself ... all the cogs and the whirring of motors.

Dark Black

October 13, 1973 — Day 37

Late tonight I saw something surface. Black. Glistening. Larger than any sea creature I have ever witnessed in all my observations. It reflected in the waxing gibbous moon draped above the North Atlantic. At first, the creature appeared like a kelp bed, but moving, shifting, stirring.

Alive.

The only other crew member awake at this late hour was the first mate on the Evening Star. I thought to run to the wheel house, to see if he was witnessing it, too. But then I feared the creature would vanish beneath the surface the very minute I took my eyes off of it. I lifted my binoculars and turned the focusing knob with my index finger.

It was a good distance from the boat, a half mile at least, but through the binoculars, I could see a number of black arms, covered in rows of sharp-toothed suckers, thrashing about the moon-silvered water. A tremendous tentacular club rose at least forty feet into the air before crashing back down into the cold ocean with a tremendous splash.

And then, briefly, I saw the massive mantle, and the eye of the tremendous beast, rising very slightly on the surface of the water, before vanishing with a shot to the deeps.

And then, all was calm.

My first thought was I had just witnessed, as impossible as it may be, a surface sighting of a very rare, totally elusive, mythic, giant squid.

Architeuthis Dux.

But as I lowered my binoculars, I realized something. The creature was far too big. At least one hundred feet from my estimation from tentacular club to the stabilizing fins on the beak.

And it wasn't flush with silver and coral color, like so many artist's renderings over the centuries had depicted, but, instead, it was midnight black, inkwell black, darker than a raven, darker than a sky with no stars, darker than anything I had ever seen in my life.

Dark black.

The rolling North Atlantic, rising and falling, rising and falling, was quiet for the rest of the night and morning. I stood on the deck of the Evening Star *for hours, hoping to see it again, hoping it would return so I could get a better look, to take some photographs.*

The sea was quiet the rest of the night, save for the arched backs of the minke whales I was there to observe in the first place. The creature, I had seen, whatever it was, never returned.

~~~

Dr. Gerald Clarke closed the small leather-bound log book and held it in his hands. He sat alone in the living room, in a cozy oak rocking chair, bathed in the warm amber light of a mission-style Tiffany lamp.

How many times over the years had he revisited that same page—day thirty-seven of his expedition aboard the *Evening Star*? It was the very beginning of his career. An earnest marine biology doctoral student studying the feeding habits of minke whales aboard a research vessel in the north Atlantic. He went on to become one of the world's great authorities on the species. But what he witnessed that night had always vexed him. It had quietly consumed him. It had remained his secret obsession, far more than the marine mammal his career was built upon. But he dared never to tell any of his mentors or colleagues over the years. He couldn't tell anyone what he had seen. No. That would have been scientific heresy. There was that one instance, that one moment he had too many pints of beer at a cavernous, low-ceilinged pub in Saint John's while the juke box played "Night Moves" and he mentioned the creature, the sea beast, for that is what it was, to a visiting professor from the United Kingdom. The man's bespectacled eyes widened and a smile emerged underneath his thick, white broom mustache and he said: "Why, Dr. Clarke! Perhaps you should come to the highlands of Scotland and start hunting for Nessie!" and he cackled.

Dr. Clarke never mentioned the sighting again to any of his peers. He shared the story with Camille, his wife of thirty-two years and she said she believed him. But cancer took Camille to the grave and took the secret with her. He told his daughter, Elisabeth, when she was old enough to understand. She believed him, too. He was her papa, after all.

But they were the only ones.

When he was out in the North Atlantic on surveys he always looked for it, stayed up later than the other scientists and crew, hoping. But he never again encountered the creature he had seen that cold autumn night so long ago.

And here he was, seventy-three-years-old, widowed, in his first year of retirement. Dr. Clarke still planned on attending conferences, publishing papers, and staying active in the world of marine biology and academe. But as he spent more days alone, cultivating his backyard vegetable garden (award-winning heirloom tomatoes), embarking on long, glorious strolls with his dog Cousteau (Havanese/Wheatan terrier), taking evening cooking classes (Korean, Vietnamese, Chinese), reading books (Oliver Sacks, Stephen Jay Gould, Loren Eisley, Dr. Seuss); listening to classical music (he favored Russian compositions: Tchaikovsky, Rachmaninov, Stravinsky), he found himself thinking more and more about his brief encounter with the sea beast on that dark night.

What was it? What had he seen?

In his solitude, he thought a lot about this. And he had an idea, as far-fetched and implausible as it may be.

And so, over the years, when he was out in the field with other scientists, in those same cold Atlantic waters, a day's journey north, he often deployed deep-sea autonomous recording devices or a range of hydrophones, hoping to pick up any sounds the creature might produce. He knew the low-frequency, repetitive grunt and thump pulses of the minkes he had studied for decades. Sometimes, and he never told anyone this, he even suspected he could occasionally understand what it was they were communicating.

Of course, Dr. Clarke knew also that cephalopods, predatory marine animals that included the giant squid, were not believed to make sounds. But what Dr. Clarke had seen that night was not a giant squid. He was now more and more certain of this.

Autumn had moved in with unusual ferocity upon Newfoundland, perhaps a harbinger of a harsh winter ahead. Saint John was a bit quieter now, more still. Dr. Clarke liked this. The tourists on the cruise ships weren't coming into town with the same daily retail shopping fervor. School children had returned to their classrooms and their desks and the droning monotony of education. Most of the old frame houses in town were now buttoned up for the coming dark, cold months, the latitude-truncated days, storm doors and storm windows in place, boilers and furnaces readied for the meteorological onslaught.

He walked with Cousteau to the cemetery where Camille was buried, walking through the creaky iron entrance gates with the pointy spikes, past the dozens of time-worn graves where the British Loyalists had been laid to rest. The collar of his Navy pea-coat upturned, he placed a bouquet of autumn lilies upon Camille's grave and stood over it and closed his eyes as the wind whipped up brittle leaves at his feet. Sometimes he could hear her words in his mind if he listened closely enough. He could hear her and understand her words the same way he listened to the minkes; the same way some listened to the word of God.

Far in the distance, a bell clanged in the harbor.

"Go," she instructed him. Simple as that.

Go.

He walked home, Cousteau sniffing every scent, lifting his leg long after he had anything left within him to leave his mark, to say he had been there.

When he returned home, he poured a glass of milk, prepared a sandwich, and with *Piano Concerto No. 2* playing in the background, he called Elisabeth to tell her he was going out to sea for a few days.

"Okay, papa. I love you. Be safe," she said, her own children making noises and distracting her.

Part of his retirement arrangement with the university was retaining access to one of the research lab's boats—*The Argo*, a former commercial fishing vessel, to continue his data collection. He packed a small duffel with a few heavy Donegal sweaters, Carhart overalls, rubber boots, a watch cap, heavy gloves.

As he prepped, he realized he had not uploaded the contents from the last recording device he had brought up from the depths of the Atlantic. He had been recording the sounds for so long, for so many years, with nary an anomalous oceanic murmur, he no longer had the same urgency he had felt as a young scientist seeking a bio-acoutician's proof that a great and epic sea beast, the creature he had seen with his very own eyes, navigated the depths of the Atlantic.

The night before Dr. Clarke departed on *The Argo*, he uploaded the data from the last autonomous deep-sea recording device and ran the application that scanned for sonic activity.

And there it was. Loud and clear as a bell in a small town on Sunday.

He was incredulous.

A screeching, a song, clicking, pulses, thumping, a repetitive clarion call. A call across all of the dark Atlantic and across the universe. It was all there on his laptop, graphic spikes of sounds repeating and repeating and repeating like scales in song.

Dr. Clarke put on his head phones and listened to it again and again. It was speaking. Talking. It was there.

The next day, the sky wraps of gauze and gray, he headed out alone from the harbor, piloting *The Argo* out to sea, bearing north.

The Argo was a scrappy, thirty-six-foot, sea-worn ship that had served a long life as a commercial haddock fishing boat. The university purchased *The Argo* at a bargain a decade ago for research. She had a reliable one-hundred-seventy-five horse power engine and room to sleep three comfortably below deck.

The winds were strong and the waters choppy, but *The Argo* dieseled north, going against the strong Labrador current. Dr. Clarke was headed to the exact coordinates where he had witnessed the creature back in 1973.

As evening descended, moving north along the coast of Newfoundland, he passed the Belle Isle Lighthouse, casting its white flash every ten seconds out to sea. Well after nightfall he arrived and cut the engine. The sky above had cleared, crisp and cold and awash in a field of sharp starlight. It was peak time for the aurora borealis and the sky did not disappoint, monstrous shifting ribbons of emerald light, swelling and receding, spiraling, flowing, a glowing representation of the universe alive.

The Argo rose up and down in the cresting water. Dr. Clarke looked out at the Atlantic, facing east. There was not another soul in sight. No one for probably one hundred miles. Not a single soul to be seen.

He knew he had to be patient. He knew the odds of seeing anything on this night were slim. He had travelled here many times in the last decades and not once did he have an encounter. It was forty-five years ago to this very night that he had seen it. And, now, all these years later, he believed he had heard it, too. He had listened to the recording over and over again on his laptop, with his headphones and the volume turned all the way up. He had never heard anything like it. It was unlike the pulses and thumps of the minke, or the clicks of dolphins, or any of the whale songs new-age composers occasionally set to synthesized songs.

He stood on the deck of *The Argo*.

"Here I am," he muttered. He was alone, he didn't have to hide his words or his belief in the creature. It was just Dr. Clarke here tonight, and the stars and the aurora, and, he hoped, the creature.

It was not a giant squid. Not Architeuthis Dux. No. Perhaps it was part of the same cephalopod class, but a new species altogether. What he had seen in 1973 had eight arms and two tentacles and a bullet-shaped mantle and eyes the size of tractor trailer tires. But it was not a giant squid. It was too large. Twenty-first century science had begun, at long last, to decipher Architeuthis Dux, a few had washed ashore, a few had been filmed, silver, white, orange, gray and, at best, fifty feet. But what he had seen was the color of Poe's inkwell and at least one hundred feet in length. What he had seen was more than a giant squid, mythology-made manifest.

It was known in Norwegian and Icelandic myth. Perhaps related to sightings of giant squid, but larger, more ominous, able to wrangle a powerful sea-faring vessel beneath the roiling sea in a crash of timber and mast.

It was the stuff of legend and nightmare.

Pen and ink renderings over the years were numerous of the great sea beast, with its tentacles and arms clutching vast ships in its midnight grip.

Dr. Clarke looked at the shifting Atlantic. No, what he had seen was not Architeuthis Dux, but its biggest brethren, a cephalopod offspring known well across the ages.

The Kraken.

And Dr. Gerald Clarke had a recording of its voice.

Before his trip, he played it over and over. And now, he suddenly understood what it was saying. It was the same way he heard Camille's voice and her words.

In the thumps and pings, shrieks and chatter, the Kraken asked the same question again and again. It was aware of him, aware of his deep-sea recording devices. It knew he had been looking and waiting. And there, on that recording it had but one question for Dr. Clarke:

What is your reason for being?

Suddenly, something struck *The Argo*, shifting the ship, moving it with no effort ninety degrees across the water as easily as a child lifts a toy. Dr. Clarke lost his footing, falling hard on his hip, pain coursing through him instantly.

And then things went still, the aurora playing in greens and blues above him. He lay on the deck, arms and legs outstretched, staring at the ribbons of light.

He sat up and braced his hand on the railing and steadied himself. He stood and his leg buckled. He looked out at the sea and there it was, in the distance and the night.

The arms moved on the surface of the water, the mantle elevated just enough to see its eyes.

And then it darted below the surface faster than any creature of that size should be able to move. Gone in an instant and all went silent once more.

He stared out at the cold calm.

"My reason for being?" he said aloud.

The ocean stayed still. He hoped the creature would return. To listen.

"My reason?" he called.

The waves heaved up and down.

"I would like to know you."

Dr. Clarke turned from the water. He had heard it. Seen it. Wincing, he limped slowly across the deck towards the wheelhouse.

As he moved, he heard a deep thump on the deck of *The Argo* and then a slick slithering.

And then he felt something, something thick and strong, coiling around his ankle, circling up his leg.

Acknowledgments

Profound gratitude to the folks who made this book happen. First and foremost, my family, Jan and the girls, Mai-Linh, Le-Anh, and Gia-Binh. Thank you for your patience with me, and your belief in these stories. And, of course, Teddy. I love you all so much.

JC Gabel, visionary, punk rock publishing provacateur, friend and mighty collaborator. Thank you for seeing exactly what I wanted to do with this book and for expanding upon this vision as only you could do. And to the entirety of the Hat & Beard team—especially Sybil Perez—thank you. To the amazing Sabrina Che for the book design.

Massive thanks to Dan Grzeca, the perfect artist to bring these stories to illustrative life. What a joy to work with such originality and talent.

To my rock 'n' roll mates, Ginger Wildheart and Scott Sorry. Thank you for the seismic inspiration.

To my literary agents, Judith Erhlich and Sophia Siedner, thank you for your guidance.

To the others who have helped me out along the way: Amy Bailey, Mort and Jane Castle, Andy Burnside-Weaver, Tom Dieboldt, and my amazing Dad.

And to you, the one holding this book, reading these words. Heartfelt gratitude. Thank you.

About the Author

Sam Weller is a two-time Bram Stoker Award-winning writer and the authorized biographer of the late Ray Bradbury. He teaches in the MFA program at Columbia College Chicago. Learn more at www.samweller.net or find Sam on Twitter @Sam__Weller

About the Artist

Dan Grzeca is an artist from Chicago. He has produced hundreds of prints, music posters, and illustrations out of his studio Ground Up Press. His work can be found at www.dangrzeca.com and @jetsah on Instagram.